SKYRIDER'S GAMBLE

"I'll take those odds," I said. They all turned to look at me in surprise. It wasn't polite to interrupt, but I've never been much good at waiting.

"Look. The longer we take getting out to Station Newhome, the more time the terrorists have to figure out we're coming. The hostages' lives are already forfeit. We know what the C.I.D. would like to do: blast the station out of space with hostages and terrorists all on board. The mission is the *only* chance they have. If we don't go, they die. If we go, and fail, they die. But if we go, and succeed, they live. It's as simple as that. . . ."

***FIRST BATTLE* by Melisa C. Michaels**
The second high-stakes SKYRIDER adventure.

MELISA C. MICHAELS

FIRST BATTLE

A TOM DOHERTY ASSOCIATES BOOK

FIRST BATTLE

First printing: November 1985

A TOR Book

Published by Tom Doherty Associates
49 West 24 Street
New York, N.Y. 10010

Cover art by Bruce Jensen

ISBN: 0-812-54568-0
CAN. ED.: 0-812-54569-9

Printed in the United States of America

To four who, one way and another, rescued me:
Florence, Peter, and my cousins Rob and Becky.

PROLOGUE

In the years since humanity began to move outward from Earth, colonizing first space stations, then the moon, then Mars, and finally the asteroid belt, a genetic mutation has developed that divides the human race into three major categories: freefall mutants, gravity tolerants, and heterozygotes (also called, respectively, "Fallers," "Grounders," and "Floaters," which see). Gravity tolerants are, of course, the original strain: able to survive periods of freefall in space, but requiring regular periods in gravity to maintain perfect health, we are the normal *homo sapiens* as evolved on Earth. The mutation for freefall tolerance first appeared on Station Challenger (see entry, pp. 16009-16010) in the middle of the twenty-first century; and although the mutation is not genetically dominant, it spread quickly throughout the colonies. Not all the potential hazards were obvious to the people of the time, who therefore welcomed the mutants' abilities to work out their lives in freefall

situations with no recourse to gravity. When heterozygotes (those having one gene for the gravity trait
and one for the freefall trait) resulted from intermar-
riages between the mutants and normal humans, the
new variety was again welcomed: the new "Floaters," as they were called due to their ability to
"float" from one environment to the other, may
have seemed the ideal solution to the problems of
living in space, since they are equally well able to
survive gravity, freefall, and frequent transitions between the two. What was not foreseen was that both
they and the freefall mutants would eventually turn
against their ancestral home, attempting to overthrow
Earth's rightful Corporate Government in a brutal
power play that resulted, in the last decade, in a
bloody police action (see "Colonial Incident," p.
3805) that, although the insurrection was successfully
put down, it cost Earth severely in terms of energy,
economy, and human resources. . . .

—*Encyclopedia Terra*

A war has been fought, but the issues are not
resolved. Grounders control the Solar System now,
and they think they own it: but I will live to see the
day when all peoples, be they Floaters or Fallers or
even Grounders, are accorded equal rights under the
law. . . .

—Takagura
The Book of Freedom

CHAPTER ONE

Collis bounced, giggling, off the wall and into his adoptive father's arms. Since his father was out of reach of any convenient walls or handholds at the time, the impact sent them tumbling head over heels across the chamber together, their laughter echoing.

"If you two idiots don't stop playing and start getting ready," I said, "we'll be late for the party."

They came to rest in a jumble of arms and legs near the doorway where I was floating with Collis's jumpsuit in one hand and Jamin's dress tunic in the other. Skyrider, maid and babysitter, at your service. It wasn't a role in which I was entirely comfortable, but even an outlaw queen has to help with the housework sometimes.

Jamin untangled himself from his son with a quick grin at me. Since they were both then upside down with respect to me and what built-in fixtures there were in the chamber, he casually snagged Collis with one hand and a freefall handhold with the other, flipped himself and the boy over with an easy grace that brought them to a halt just in front of me, and said cheerfully, "Isn't this a party?"

"Sure it is." But I couldn't help returning his grin. Hell, it *was* fun watching the kid get accustomed to freefall. I'd had enough of watching the two of them try to coexist in gravity. Jamin was a Faller: gravity was agony to him. Collis was a Grounder, with an inner ear problem that made him dangerously ill in freefall before the med-techs finally came up with a drug that seemed to work.

Collis swarmed out of Jamin's grip in an unpracticed grab for his jumpsuit that got him his clothing but left him floating gently off toward the center of the chamber. "Bother." He flailed his arms and legs uselessly, giggled again, and curled into a ball around the jumpsuit in his arms. "I keep doing that."

"Every action has an equal and opposite reaction," said Jamin.

Collis grinned impishly. "Yes, but how do you know which way you'll go?"

I tried to look stern, which was particularly difficult to do while watching Collis wrestle with his clothing. "We won't go anywhere if you don't get dressed."

He looked at me, briefly uncertain whether I was really cross with him. "I didn't know freefall would be so fun."

"You still don't feel sick?" asked Jamin.

"Nah," said Collis, with a six-year-old's total disdain. " 'Course not. The med-techs *fixed* that."

Jamin left his dress tunic in the air beside him while he stripped off his work tunic and put it in the cleaner. "They didn't fix it. They're experimenting on you."

"Jamin," I said.

His quick blue eyes glanced my way and his sudden, unexpected grin transformed the dark lean lines of his face. "I know, I know. It's not their fault his condition is inoperable."

"And they're doing the best they can," said Collis. "Skyrider, oh, bother, look, I've lost my darned old slipper again."

The offending slipper was floating lazily toward a far corner of the chamber. I, hotshot Skyrider, daredevil pilot of the asteroids, dutifully kicked off after it, glad no one was there but Jamin and Collis to see me on duty as surrogate mother. It would have ruined my reputation. "Just let the dirty jumpsuit go," I said, because he was trying to hold onto it and put on his clean one at the same time. "I'll stuff it in the cleaner for you."

"Oh, thanks." Collis released his grip on the jumpsuit he had taken off and bemusedly watched it float beside him. "Papa, what's a summit meeting?"

I snagged the slipper, floated toward Collis to hand it to him, and caught his discarded jumpsuit. He looked up from his struggles to flash me a quick, grateful smile.

"Just a meeting of government people," said Jamin. Even in freefall, where he was comfortable, he looked startlingly serious, even somber, beside his cheerful blue-eyed boy.

"Well, why don't they say that? Why do they say 'summit'?" asked Collis.

"I suppose because they're top officials. You know, a summit is the top of something."

"Will the President of the whole World, Incorporated really be there?"

"She said she would. Look out, you're going to hit the bulkhead."

Collis got his legs in his jumpsuit and put out a hand to ward off the wall. "It's a wall, Papa. In a space station, bulkheads are walls."

"That depends," said Jamin.

Collis braced his feet against the disputed object and slipped his arms into the jumpsuit. "Depends on what?"

"On who's talking," said Jamin.

"Well, then, I'm talking," Collis said with satisfaction, "and I call it a wall."

"So much for summit meetings," I said.

"Why, are they about walls?" asked Collis.

"Not usually. But they are for settling disputes. Like whether it's a wall or a bulkhead. And this particular summit meeting is between Earthers, who call all bulkheads walls; and Colonists, who call most walls bulkheads. Colonists don't have walls at all, except on planets or asteroids."

He looked at me. "You do, though."

"Hell, I've been known to have walls in a ship. I was raised on Earth, don't forget." And I still had relatives there, which until recently had given me a bad case of divided loyalties; but events had changed that, rather finally.

"Why'd you run away, then?"

"From Earth you mean?

burc." He got his jumpsuit fastened and tried one of his father's cat flips, apparently intending to get the same side up as I was. He gave it too much thrust, though, and kept tumbling. "Bother."

I caught him and a handhold, and got us more or less stationary beside the door. "I don't exactly remember. It was a long time ago."

"Didn't you like Earthers?"

"Some of my best friends were Earthers."

Jamin made a sound like strangled laughter. "Those are fighting words."

"Why?" asked Collis.

"You're certainly full of questions today," said Jamin.

"I'm excited," said Collis.

"If you're also dressed," I said, "we'd best go now." It wasn't that I was in a hurry to get to the party, so much as that I was in a hurry to get the worst over with as quickly as possible. Social gatherings have never been one of my favorite things. At least, not formal social gatherings.

"I'm dressed," said Collis. "Papa, you're upside down."

Jamin looked up from fastening his tunic. "No, you're upside down."

"Am I? How do you tell?"

"He was teasing you, squirt," I said. "Nobody's upside down, or maybe we all are. There's no way to tell. Though maybe I should warn you, before we get to the party, that the people who get there first establish which side up the party will be: it's considered polite for late-comers to turn the same side up as the people already there."

"You mean people won't float around any old side up?"

"Usually not. And a lot of the people at this party are going to be as unfamiliar with freefall as you are, so don't go bouncing off the walls and knocking anybody over, or anything."

"I won't."

"Okay, let's go." I let go his hand and gave him a little shove into the corridor. Jamin passed me while

I was regaining my balance; then I joined them, and we propelled ourselves along by handholds toward the ballchamber where the party was being held for the bored wives and families of VIPs attending the summit meeting.

I don't know whose bright idea the party was. I suppose it wasn't that bad an idea, in itself. Nobody could have foreseen how it would turn out. At the time, I thought it would just be awkward; the political atmosphere was tense, at best, and even wives and families have opinions. Maybe in a party environment they'd be too polite to say anything; but Jamin and Collis and I were smack in the middle of the controversy, and I didn't think they'd all be glad to see us.

We had helped save a passenger liner named the *Marabou*. Nobody found fault with that. What they didn't like was our accusation as to who sabotaged her in the first place. The thing had been set up to look like the work of Colonial Insurrectionists, but by the time we got to her we were pretty sure the people behind it were actually Earthers. That was confirmed when Earther pilots in Patrol Starbirds, rather clumsily overpainted with the blazon of the Colonial Fleet, tried to keep us from bringing her in.

We had witnesses on the *Marabou*, including a Board Advisor and a number of media people who took holofilms of the battle in progress. Unfortunately, the real Colonial Warriors who helped us ward off the Patrol did their job a little too well. We couldn't find any identifiable debris afterward, and the Company was trying to pass off our accusation as political propaganda. They didn't quite call it a hoax, but they wanted to. Failing that, they'd have quietly

spaced the whole affair if we'd had no witnesses with
Board Advisor Brown's political influence.

The summit meeting was a result of her efforts.
She thought that if the Earther and Colonial VIPs all
got together to discuss the incident, some mutually
satisfactory resolution might be found that would
forestall active hostilities. I wouldn't have bet rockdust
on the side of the good guys, but I never claimed to
understand politics. It tries my patience. Show me a
shuttle and I'll show you how to fly it, but don't ask
me to sit still in a room full of talkers who won't say
what they mean, and won't mean what they say.
That's how I see politicians, and I'm too likely to
take a swipe at the first one who gets smart with me.
Which is frowned on, in some circles.

Board Advisor Brown wasn't like that. I liked her.
And while my inclination was still to blast Earth's
VIP City off the face of the planet, it didn't cost
anything to try her way, first. The Company even
paid me to ferry some of their VIPs up from Earth.

The summit meeting, and, by extension, the party
we were attending, took place in a freefall station,
because many of the Colonial VIPs were Fallers like
Jamin. It was one of the complaints Colonials had
with the Company. Why should we be governed by
Grounders, from a planet half the Colonial popula-
tion couldn't even visit? They didn't understand our
needs or our lives or our people, and they didn't
really think Fallers were quite human. Why should
we pay taxes to, and obey the laws of, people like
that? Of course, not all of us did pay taxes or obey
the laws. . . .

"Hey, hotshot." Jamin pushed at the door to the
ballchamber, looking back at me, and absently snagged
his son when the boy inadvertently floated on past.

"I forgot to give you Board Advisor Brown's message."

"What message?" I caught a handhold and balanced next to him, watching Collis try to bounce off a wall.

"She said to tell you to control your temper. No, listen, I'm just repeating what she said." He grinned maliciously. "She said she wasn't sure she could bail you out, if you started a brawl with some Earther VIP's smart-mouthed relative. Your reputation precedes you, as always."

"Did she say anything about smart-mouthed Fallers?"

"She didn't mention them."

"Then you might bear in mind, rock jockey, that I've refrained from killing you, so far, only because I'd have had an unfair advantage in gravity."

"There's no gravity here."

"Just so." We eyed each other, calculating.

"You guys," said Collis, bouncing impatiently between us. "Come on, I want to go to the party."

CHAPTER TWO

I am not fond of crowds. In a gathering of Belters I do okay; we're a rough and ready crew and what tacit rules of behavior there are don't extend to the sort of thing Earthers refer to as "good manners." While I don't generally give a damn what people think of me, I do like to think well of myself. In a Belter crowd, that's easy. I know how to act, and I know I can take on anybody who doesn't like how I act. Hotshot Skyrider, risk taker, law breaker. Sure, it's immature. It's also fun.

Among Earthers I'm not so confident. I feel awkward and out of place. Particularly when the Earthers include women. I don't want to wear dresses and giggle behind fans, but for some damn reason I feel like a barbarian when I'm the only woman in the place who *doesn't* wear dresses and giggle behind fans. Or even one of only a few who don't.

I know I really look okay: I've been told that by most standards I'm even pretty; and while the customary Belter costume of tunic, stretch pants, slippers, and side arm wasn't designed for pretty, it looks well enough on me. Still I'd caught myself feeling grateful, as I got ready for this party, that in freefall surely even Earther women would have sense enough not to wear their elegant, entangling dresses.

What I hadn't foreseen was that they'd find a way to look delicate and dainty in costumes designed for freefall. I'm small, but I felt like a whacking great clod of primitive clumsiness the moment we entered the ballchamber. Earther women don't just neglect to wear side arms: they manage to give the impression, without ever saying a word, that any female who does wear one is in a class with the chimpanzees they breed for labor on Mars. As for the rest of my costume— Well, they pretended to be polite about it.

Nobody had been fool enough to wear a dress to the party, but the Earther women had designed a sort of flowing jumpsuit that managed to look like a dress without being one. It came in all colors, sizes, and shapes, with variations in fabric, trim, neckline, and accoutrements, all of them elegant. They were resplendent. And they carried the inevitable fans.

Well, hell. If I didn't giggle, I wouldn't need a fan. Since I very seldom giggle, I saw no particular reason why I'd suddenly get an overwhelming impulse to do so here, in a crowd of strangers, so many of whom were potential if not actual enemies.

The chamber had a door in every wall, including the ones that would have been floor and ceiling if there were gravity to determine which was which. We entered by one that was nominally ''above'' the people there before us—which is to say, we came in wrong side up. The novelty of it delighted Collis, who showed a tendency to loiter head-first in the

doorway, staring happily at the bright gathering of
party-dressed people with their bodies all more or
less aligned as though the wall opposite us were the
floor. "How do we get down there without bumping
anybody?" he asked.

"Very carefully." I didn't feel quite competent to
quibble with his use of the word "down," just then.

Jamin said, "And try to see that if you do any
bumping, it's not with your feet, okay?"

"Sure," said Collis. "That would be kicking. Everybody knows that's not okay except for fighting."

"And no fighting," said Jamin.

Collis glanced at him. "Who do you mean? Me,
or the Skyrider?"

"Both." A wry grin twisted his lips. "With two
hotshots along—"

"Watch your mouth, rock jockey." I flipped over
and gave myself a leisurely shove toward the party.
"We're here to have fun, remember?"

"Unfortunately, I also remember what the average
Belter considers fun." He helped Collis turn over,
and floated alongside him to ward off disasters. "In
the Outer Rocks—"

"Space the Outer Rocks." I was almost on a level
with the main body of partygoers. "Jamin, damn it,
if I can't get through this without a fight, I wish at
least it wouldn't be with you."

He glanced at me, sharply. "Whatsamatta you?
Nervous?"

Naturally, I denied it. "And don't go dropping
into pidgin like that. It'll make the Earthers nervous."

"You must be from the asteroid belt," said a
glittering lady to my right. "My goodness, how exciting. *Do* speak pidgin if you like; I've never heard

it.'' She said it as though she were granting us a favor.

"Thanks very much, but we'll stick to Company English.'' I glanced at Collis as I said it.

The woman leaned back to look at me. "Well.'' She took in every aspect of my costume, letting her gaze linger a moment on the side arm strapped to my hip. "I'd always heard most Belters couldn't speak Company English.'' It was almost an accusation.

"Some can, some can't. Same like Earthers.''

"Same like.'' She repeated it too loudly. "How quaint. Is that pidgin? I'd always understood that pidgin was unintelligible to an English speaker.''

I admit I clenched my fist, but I didn't use it. "Some is, some isn't. It's an argot, really, made up of all the languages brought out by the early pioneers. But if you want information on languages, I suggest you consult your *Encyclopedia Terra*; I'm no expert.''

"My dear, your English is excellent.'' Her tone said how surprised she was by that.

Collis bumped into me, knocking me away from the Earther woman. I suspected his father of giving him a shove to get him there, but I was too busy preventing the collision from spreading to worry about it then. "Skyrider, where's the drinks and things?'' Collis squirmed out of my arms without quite kicking anyone.

At the sound of my too well known nickname, several heads turned our way, including that of the glittering lady who had condescended to speak to me. "Skyrider,'' she said. "Well. No wonder.''

I edged Collis toward the nearest tray of refreshments. Someone asked Jamin, behind me, "Is that really the Skyrider?''

"Are those tube things the drinks?" asked Collis.

"Don't sound so incredulous. What did you expect, glasses and bottles?"

"I guess I did. But they'd spill, wouldn't they?"

"Spill would be one word." The tray and its contents were held in place by a portable gravity generator with a very narrow field. "What do you want, soda pop?"

"Yes, please. Red, if they have it."

They had red. I gave it to him, and took a caffeine for myself. We were just turning away from the tray when my cousin Michael came gliding out of a nearby cluster of Martians with one of his sons in tow. "Melacha?" He had calculated his glide precisely to bring him up next to the tray of refreshments. "I thought I saw you come in. Is this Collis?"

Collis stared. Michael was wearing a Martian flight suit, with all his decorations from the war neatly arrayed over the pocket. "Are you a Colonial Warrior?" Collis asked, in awe.

Michael grinned. He looked as mischievous as the freckle-faced boy I had known twenty years ago on Earth, whose favorite pastime had been tormenting girl cousins. "I was." He emphasized the past tense. "There's officially no Colonial Fleet, these days, you know."

"Sure, but it was Colonial Fleet Starbirds that blasted the Patrol, after the Skyrider chased them away from the *Marabou*," said Collis. He looked at me. "Aren't I supposed to say that?"

"I don't see why not. That's what the whole summit meeting is about: whether those were Patrol boats or Colonial Warriors." I looked at Michael. "I think this was one of the real Warriors, who saved us."

"Saved!" he said disdainfully. "*You* saved us."

Then he realized what I'd said, and stared again at Michael. "Oh, were you, really? Did you do that? Were you there, did you see the battle?"

"I saw." Michael tugged his son forward. "Melacha, Collis, I want you to meet my oldest boy, Jeremiah."

"Jerry," said the boy.

"Jeremiah, this is Melacha Rendell, also known as the Skyrider; and Collis, son of Jamin."

"Pleased to meet you," said both boys, and then grinned at each other, shyly. They were about the same age, one red-haired and freckled, the other blond, and both a little awkward in freefall.

"That's my dad Jamin," said Collis. He gestured vaguely the way we had come. "He piloted the *Marabou.*"

"Were you on her?" asked Jerry. "Were you with the Skyrider when she dead-docked with the *Marabou?* My dad says nobody else could've done that."

"My dad could," said Collis. "He was a hero in the war."

"So was my dad," said Jerry.

Michael looked embarrassed. "Um, did you say you wanted soda pop, Jerry?" He made a move toward the tray.

"Take red," said Collis. "It's good."

Jerry took red, and Michael chased the two of them off toward where one of his wives was waiting with several more of his children. "You still listening to dead Gypsies?" he asked when they were gone.

It was my turn to look moderately embarrassed. "I can still hear them, sometimes, if that's what you mean. They saved us a couple of times on the flight out to the *Marabou.*"

"Don't sound so defensive. I'm not an Earther."

"You're not a Belter, either. And not everybody can hear ghosts."

"I think you'll find most Martians can. Whatsamatta you? People give you trouble about it?"

"It's part of the legend, I guess. You know. The Great Skyrider. People are bound to look at me a little funny, when they've heard some of the stories."

"We could use that legend," he said seriously.

"We? Use it?"

"I wish you'd join us."

"What are you, a recruiting officer for the Colonial Fleet or something?"

"Not so loud. That's one of my jobs. And we could use people like you and Jamin. The legends would be good for morale."

I was shaking my head before he'd finished. "No. No, Michael. I ain't no hero. Or a warrior. No."

He studied me. "Planning to sit this one out, too?"

Obviously he thought I'd take a swing at him for that. But why should I? That, too, was part of the legend: the lady who couldn't make up her mind. I'd sat out the last war, telling myself it was too far away and none of my business. This time it was going to reach out to the asteroid belt, and I knew it. And it damn well was my business. But I didn't have to admit that, yet. I grinned at him. "Maybe I will. Wanta make something of it?"

He looked sheepish as he dropped the defensive posture he'd automatically assumed. "Not really." He took a tube of caffeine from the tray, squeezed a glob of it into the air before him, and leaned forward to catch it in his mouth. "What are you waiting for?"

"Waiting?"

"Before you commit yourself."

I shrugged. "Maybe just a good enough offer. I'm a mercenary. I work for a living. Make it worth my while, and maybe I will join your little army."

"Till somebody else makes you a better offer?"

He looked like he thought I might hit him for that one, too, but I just grinned. "Sure. What else?"

"I suppose you sneer at words like honor, freedom, and independence?"

"Hell, no. I'm as independent as they come."

"As long as the Patrol doesn't catch you."

"As long as the Patrol doesn't catch me." I grinned. "I've got a good thing going. Why should I sign on to follow somebody else's orders? I don't like taking orders."

"I guess that's fine, if you can get away with it."

"I can."

"Not everybody has that freedom."

"That's their problem. Why should I come running to the aid of a bunch of slobs who can't take care of themselves?"

"Why did you run to the aid of the *Marabou*?"

I stared. "Well, space, didn't you know? That's how I got my Falcon. Did you think I did it for free?"

"Okay, why do you smuggle in goods to the freelancers and farmers?"

"That pays quite well. Smuggling usually does."

"Even Rat Johnson?"

Rat Johnson was a beady-eyed old Gypsy who'd been mining his little rock longer than I'd been flying. He seldom paid for his supplies, he had no synch system, and his section of the Belt had more wild rocks than anywhere else I'd been. "I've been supplying him too long to stop now," I said. "Hell, he's an investment. When he hits that vein of malite he's been looking for, we'll both be rich.''

"There's no malite on that rock, and you know it.''

"Besides, dodging rocks is good practice. So is dead-docking, come to that. If I hadn't been supplying Rat for so many years, I'd never have been able to dock with the *Marabou*.''

"You have an answer for everything, haven't you?''

"I hope so.''

He grinned suddenly. "Well, come on over and meet the wife and kids, anyway.''

I'd have liked to, but I never got the chance: I had just opened my mouth to answer him when a woman on the far side of the chamber screamed. It wasn't a playful party scream. It was real fear.

CHAPTER THREE

Stun guns are completely silent. If you're on the wrong end of one, you can't tell whether it's working till you see someone fall. If it hits you, you never know it was working till you wake up. Even then you have to be told; you don't remember what happened. Of course, if you've been hit by one before, you can make a good guess based on the intensity of the headache you wake up with.

The terrorists had theirs set for spray. In a freefall environment, stunned people don't fall down, but the choked-off scream of a terrified Earther woman was just as telling: and when the whole cluster of people nearest her suddenly went limp and began to float gently and aimlessly apart, that clinched it.

I saw the terrorists who shot her, but like most of the Belters present, I stayed where I was, with my hand well away from my side arm: I'd heard another group come in through the door behind me, and I don't much like getting stunned.

27

Michael moved. Most of the Earthers were trying to get away from the terrorists, which wasn't easy, since the party was surrounded. Michael, not being an Earther, wasn't quite that stupid. But Mars is almost as civilized as Earth, and the war was several years past. He might have made a fine warrior once, but in peacetime his reflexes had gone bad. He went for his weapon.

If he hadn't dived toward the farther group of terrorists at the same time, he'd have been knocked right out. As it was, the stun caught him at an angle. He lost his weapon, and control of his dive, but he didn't lose consciousness.

His eyes watched me. I had to ignore him; I was busy counting terrorists. There were three groups of them, and the two groups I could see without turning my head were dressed in what appeared to be cast-off uniforms, mostly Colonial. One woman had on a Patrol flight suit, with a Colonial Warrior badge pasted where the Patrol badge had been when the suit was new. They spoke pidgin to each other, like Belters, but they moved like Earthers, and they fired like Earthers.

Only an Earther could fire into a crowded hall like that without giving a damn who got hit, and whether there were kids among the victims. There'd been two kids in the first group hit. I could see them floating, limp and helpless, past a group of Belters who looked as though they wanted to do something and knew they'd better not. Stunning is harder on kids. If those two didn't get medical attention soon, they might die of it.

But I didn't have time to worry about that, either. I thought I'd located all the terrorists now, without getting singled out for their attention, myself. There were six in the group that stunned the kids: four men and two women. Behind me, where I'd just caught a brief glimpse over my shoulder, there were three in the group that had stunned Michael. Those were all women. The third group, a half dozen or so, were floating overhead, in the doorway through which Collis, Jamin, and I had entered the chamber. Those were mostly men, and were the most shabbily dressed of the lot. They were also the most dangerous-looking, perhaps only because they looked the most like Earthers. From there they had a good view of everything that went on. But the chamber was a large one; even half a dozen of them couldn't see everything at once.

An Earther asked, in a voice that was trying to sound calm, "What do you want?"

The woman in the Patrol suit laughed. One of the men beside her took time to frown at her before he said, "Everybody stay calm, and you won't get hurt."

Someone else said, "But what do you want?"

I gave a furtive little kick at the wall beneath me that set me floating gently at an angle, toward the door on the side wall, away from any of the terrorists. Collis was still with Michael's family, but I couldn't see Jamin anywhere, and I couldn't look very actively, since I was trying not to draw attention to my own movements. If I could get to the side door, and safely out it, I'd have a chance at getting the real Patrol there in time to stop the terrorists from whatever they were trying to do; or, failing that, I might have a chance at stopping them myself, though that would be tough to do, in a chamberful of inexperienced Earthers whose reactions to danger and violence were unpredictable at best.

"We want a few of you to come along with us,"

said the woman in the Patrol suit. She pointed to an
Earther. "You. And you." She's pointed to a second
Earther. Both of them looked petrified with terror.

A man beside them said uncertainly, "You can't
get away with this."

The woman in the Patrol suit stunned him. Her
weapon was still set for spray, and she got two
women and another man with him, but she didn't
seem to mind that. "Anybody else got anything to
say?" she asked.

Then they were back to selecting hostages. I saw a
Belter and a Patrol officer, both armed, exchanging
signals to one side of the terrorists who were doing
the selecting. They tried to get behind the Patrol-
suited woman, who was busy choosing hostages and
didn't notice them; but one of the half dozen in the
doorway overhead saw. His weapon wasn't set on
spray. He took out the Belter first. The Patrolman,
seeing what had happened, went for his weapon, but
he never made it.

I was almost at the door when the woman selected
Michael's wife and a few of his kids, with Collis
among them. I saw Jamin, then: he'd apparently been
working his way toward Collis from across the chamber. Being a Belter, he didn't completely lose his
head when he saw Collis being herded out of the
chamber; but, being a father, he came damn close to
it. He also came damn close to getting away with it.
His dive was so swift and so sudden nobody saw him
coming till he had the woman in the Patrol suit in his
grasp. Then he was too close for them to stun him
without stunning her, too, so one of the men next to
her braced himself and walloped Jamin over the head
with the butt of a gun.

The force of the blow sent the terrorist who had

rendered it spinning out of control, despite having
braced himself. But it stopped Jamin, and the other
terrorists were prepared for anything, after that. Nobody in the crowd moved while the spinning terrorist
caught a handhold and brought himself to a stop
against the chamber wall: everybody was staring nervously down the muzzles of stun guns held poised by
terrorists who just might be rattled enough to fire for
effect.

Nobody noticed when I slipped gently and silently
out the side door. The corridor outside seemed bleak
and empty after the bright lights and glittering costumes in the ballchamber. The plasteel walls gleamed
dully, with a blurred reflection of me floating toward
a handhold. I felt a perverse longing for the dull
rock walls of home. This was hardly the time for
that. A trick of light and shadow changed my reflection into Michael's. The look he had given me as he
floated away. . . . What the hell had he expected me
to do, get myself stunned in a grandstand play, same
like him? That wouldn't have done anyone any good.

It was too late to go after the Patrol, and I didn't
like to hit an alarm; the terrorists might react by
stunning the whole party before they left. That could
be disastrous for the remaining kids and anybody in
there with a weak heart, or any of half a dozen other
medical infirmities. I put my hand on my weapon
now, but I didn't draw it. If I tried to take them in
the ballchamber, it could have the same result as
hitting an alarm.

There wasn't a Comm Link nearby from which to
call the Patrol. I didn't take time to look far for one.
In the ballchamber behind me, the terrorists had begun to herd their hostages out into a corridor around

a corner from me. My only real hope was to reach their ship before they did.

It took a moment to remember where the nearest shuttle dock was located, since I didn't think they'd use the public flight deck, crowded as it was; and another moment to decide whether the nearest was the one they would be using. It seemed a good probability. There was another, not much farther, in the opposite direction, but that one was nearer the Patrol center; and anyway, if they used it, I hadn't a hope of reaching it before them. I could reach the nearer one.

When I came up against a handhold along the way that had a Comm Link next to it, I took time to use it. The Patrol had a lot of questions I couldn't be bothered to answer. I told them, briefly, what had happened and where I was going. Even that took too much time. When I got to the shuttle dock, the terrorists were there before me. The Patrol wasn't.

I barely stopped my headlong dive in time to stay out of the corridor they were in. They had their hostages carefully spread out between them and possible points of attack. That wouldn't have done them any good with the Earth-based Patrol, but it stopped me. I wasn't about to stun a bunch of innocent partygoers, including children, in an effort to stop a batch of terrorists. Even if I tried, I probably couldn't stop them all.

I could hear them talking among themselves, no longer in pidgin. With any luck, maybe one of them would be fool enough to say where they were taking the hostages. I kept out of sight at the end of a side corridor, near enough to watch and listen without being caught, unless one of them was clever enough

to recognize for what it was the dull reflection I cast
on the far wall.

I was also near enough to see Collis's face as he
was loaded with the others onto the terrorist ship. He
was white with fear, but he hadn't given in to it.
Michael's children included one youngster half Collis's
age, a baby Michael's wife was carrying, and Jerry.
Their mother couldn't very well cope with both the
little ones at once. Collis was comforting the one she
couldn't carry. In freefall he could hold the younger
child in one arm, leaving his other hand free for
handholds, and that was what he was doing.

Beside him, Jerry was clinging to his mother's
shirt and trying not to cry. Like I said, Mars is
almost as civilized as Earth. Kids there have more time
to *be* kids. In the asteroid belt, kids grow up fast, or
maybe they don't grow up at all. The differences
were obvious in those two boys. Not that I blamed
Jeremiah for reacting the way he did. Civilized six-
year-olds simply don't cope well with crises. Why
should they?

I thought, when I saw Jeremiah's father come
tumbling down the corridor toward the landing dock,
that maybe civilized parents didn't cope very well,
either. I was as well hidden from him as I was from
the terrorists, for which I was glad; if he was crazy
enough to tackle them single-handed, he'd be crazy
enough to mix me up in it if he could.

He was still fighting the effects of the stun he'd
taken, and his coordination was bad. Maybe he could
see straight, but his arms and legs didn't seem to do
what he told them to. He banged into the wall twice
while I was watching. It didn't help that he was
clinging as if for life to an odd little black object he
was carrying. I thought at first it was a weapon, but

it didn't look like any I'd ever seen. I also thought for sure he was going to drop it when he collided with the wall, but he didn't.

I looked back at the terrorists. From where they floated, I was invisible, but Michael wasn't. And there wasn't . damn thing I could do about it; the kids were still between me and the terrorists. I thought of creating a diversion, to keep them from looking back and seeing Michael, but I couldn't think of anything that wouldn't result in a mess as dangerous as a direct attack.

They hadn't deliberately killed anyone yet. With any luck at all, when they did see Michael, they'd only stun him. Since I couldn't fire without hitting hostages, any interference I did try would only get me stunned, as well. If Michael wanted to be a damn fool, I didn't see any particular reason why I should, too. Even if I slid into the main corridor and got myself shot straight away, to keep the terrorists from noticing Michael for a few more moments, they'd see him soon enough afterward. He hadn't a hope of stopping them, any more than I had.

They'd quit making any effort to look like Colonials. Same like dropping from pidgin back into Company English, they now quit trying to look expert at freefall travel. Anybody familiar with the Belt could have told at the party that these people had never been there, and now it was more than ever obvious. But the act had served its purpose. Earthers would be all too ready to believe what they wanted to believe: and they wanted to believe that all Belters were Colonial sympathizers, that all Colonial sympathizers were Insurrectionists, and that all Insurrectionists were vicious and unprincipled warmongers.

It didn't bode well for their hostages that they

didn't maintain the act once they were out of the ballchamber. I wished they had. I wanted to believe these people had a chance to survive.

Collis was one of the last onto the ship. He pushed his luck, pausing in the hatch long enough to ask, "Where are you taking us?" I hadn't seen him look my way, or Michael's; he must just have hoped someone was listening. It was a good try, but it didn't work. The terrorists shoved him right onboard without answering.

By then, Michael had got nearer than I'd have believed possible. The terrorists weren't watching behind them as closely as they should have been; they were too busy getting the hostages loaded. Michael was coming in fast, holding that black object out before him, when they finally noticed him.

He held the black thing like a weapon, but it didn't do him a damn bit of good. As far as I could tell, he never even fired it. None of the terrorists reacted as though he had. When they saw him, one of them just calmly turned and stunned him before going on through the hatch and into the ship.

They had never given any hint where they were taking the hostages. I didn't have time to worry about it, though. Michael's trajectory, unaffected by the shot that stunned him, was taking him straight for the closing hatch. If he wasn't stopped in time, he'd be crushed; I had no doubt the terrorists would override the computer's automatic effort to stop the closing metal plates when they encountered resistance.

It was damn close, but I stopped him. As we banged up against the wall next to the hatch, I could hear the plates on the far side of the air lock snapping shut. The terrorist ship was out of reach, now, with Collis and Michael's family on it.

I just let myself bump up against the wall again, still hanging onto Michael's unconscious body, and cursed. That's what I was doing when the Patrol finally showed up. By then I'd heard the terrorist ship disengage and blast away from the station.

A Patrolwoman caught Michael's little black "weapon" out of the air where he'd dropped it. I'd forgotten it; I thought it was useless. I watched her dully for a full minute, I think, before I finally came to my senses. I was supposed to be a woman of action. I could dead-dock with a wild rock and out-fight any two other pilots in the Belt before breakfast. I'd done worse. I was the hair-trigger infighter with the scars to prove it, the cold-hearted mercenary who could and would take on the most ridiculously suicidal missions if the pay was right: and the look on a blue-eyed boy's frightened face left me cursing in the corridors when there was still a chance to go after the bastards who took him.

It wasn't the lack of a lucrative offer that slowed me: if I could get those hostages back, there'd be money in it. The plain fact was that I loved that kid. Love can be more dangerous than the laws of physics. Cursing my own stupidity, now, I loosed my hold on Michael at last and kicked away from the wall, heading for the flight deck where the *Defiance* was waiting. There was still a chance I could pick up the terrorists on my scanners, and even a small chance was better than none. If I could scan them, I could follow them.

With the Patrol present, I should have known better than to move so unexpectedly. As I've said, the Patrol is Earth-based, and filled with Earthers, who don't much care who they shoot, especially if it isn't a fellow Earther. Which I obviously wasn't.

CHAPTER FOUR

I'd been stunned a time or two in the past, so I
didn't need Jamin to tell me what had happened
when I woke up in Sick Bay with a world champion
headache. I let him tell me, though. It gave him
something to do. He looked as though if he ran out of
things to do there'd be trouble.

To keep me from floating all over Sick Bay while I
was unconscious, they'd strapped me loosely into a
hammock, and Jamin had one arm hooked over a
handhold next to it to keep him in place. From the
way he kept his arm folded hard against it, you'd
have thought it took all his strength to keep him
there. Maybe it did. He probably wanted to go
flying off in any direction, or maybe in all directions;
being environmentally incompatible didn't keep him
and his kid from being hell of close. It can't have
been easy for him to stay on that space station, doing
nothing useful, while terrorists held Collis hostage
somewhere else.

"I don't know why in space they thought they had to shoot you, on top of everything else," he said.

"They probably didn't think. It's not part of the job. And they hardly need a reason for shooting anybody, do they? They're Earthers." I put my hand on top of my head, where there was a metal plate inside to hold my brains in; a souvenir of an accident that killed someone else I loved, a long time ago. At least, it seemed long ago now, and I felt very old. I hadn't meant to love anyone, after that. "We'll get him back, Jamin."

"They won't *let* us." His voice sounded as near panic as I'd ever heard it. "You know the C.I.D.'s standard response to hostage situations."

"Who brought the C.I.D. in on this?" I knew their standard response, all right, and the thought of it chilled me right through.

"I don't know. They're just here. They won't tell me anything, though; I'm just a Faller. Oh, *Collis!*"

I'd kill to hear somebody say my name like that.

"Just hang loose. We will get him back," I said.

He shook his head bitterly. "There are limits to what even you can do."

"Nonsense." I tried to produce an encouraging grin, but with my head feeling twice its normal size and about to explode, it's possible the effort wasn't entirely successful. "Have you talked to Michael?"

He looked moderately puzzled. Just then he couldn't have looked more than moderately anything, except worried. "Michael?"

"My cousin." When that resulted in continued puzzlement, I said, "The Martian I was with. You know. At the party. It was Michael's kids Collis was with. And Michael chased the terrorists to the shuttle dock."

That was the identifying factor. "Oh, is that his name? They brought a Martian in with you. He's on the other side of the chamber." He gestured distractedly, and I loosened the strap that held me to the hammock so I could sit up to look. That was a mistake. In freefall, up and down don't make any difference, even to a headache; but movement does. "The med-techs said they'd bring something for your headache," he said.

My opinion of the promises of med-techs never got stated; Michael woke just then, and he didn't do it quietly. He must have been dreaming. Both Jamin and I started toward him at once, but the med-techs, prompt for once, got there first. I hadn't even seen them enter the chamber. They gave him a hypospray, and one of them stayed to hold him in place till it took effect, while another of them came toward me with another dose of the same stuff.

I warded her off nervously, looking past her to Michael. "What's in it?"

"Just something for the headache," she said with a med-tech's meaningless sympathy. "Hold still."

I said, "Michael?"

The med-tech at his side released him, and he floated out of his hammock toward me, still looking a little unsteady, but better than I felt. When he nodded, I let the med-tech do her stuff, and felt instantly better.

"Thank you," I said sheepishly.

She shook her head in amusement. "Belters," she said, in exactly the fondly superior tone I'd heard more than one mother use to say, "Children."

I gave it right back to her, complete with the headshake. "Earthers. First they stun you for no reason, then they wonder why you don't trust them."

She looked vaguely surprised. "But the Patrol must have had a good reason to stun you. When you break the law, you know—"

"I didn't break any laws. I tried to follow the terrorists who took hostages out of the VIP party a little while ago. Why d'you suppose the Patrol would object to that? That is, *if* the terrorists were really Colonials, and not Earthers?"

She used a convenient gravity tray to give herself a little push away from me. "Well, really!"

"Yeah. Really." I turned away in disgust. "And now it's too late to follow them."

"No it isn't," said Michael, but he didn't have time to explain his optimism. Half a dozen burly Patrolmen interrupted. Seeing we were all three out of hammocks and as healthy as could be expected under the circumstances, they solemnly surrounded us, pushing the med-techs aside.

"What's this?" asked a med-tech.

"Patrol business," said a Patrolman. "Come with us, please." He didn't mean the med-tech; he meant Michael and Jamin and me. And he didn't mean the "please," either. That was just part of the standard formula. He probably didn't even realize he'd said it.

"Where?" asked Michael.

"Just come along," said the Patrolman.

Since we were probably more accustomed to freefall than they, we might have been able to overpower them if we'd tried, and I admit I was tempted. But there was no point to it. We went along, as instructed.

Without a word, they led us out of Sick Bay and along a corridor to a junction where three corridors crossed at right angles to each other. The one they turned onto was "down" with relation to our positions when we came out of Sick Bay. As far as I could remember, the chambers in that direction were all devoted to official (read, Earther) business, which didn't bode well for us.

Before turning with them, I glanced along the other corridors, to each side and "above" us. No help there. Nobody in sight, and nothing but closed doors, as far as I could see. Sighing, I flipped into the indicated corridor, head-first toward the unknown, and had time to notice as I did so that the four Patrolmen I saw take the turn were almost as experienced in freefall as Jamin and I, despite their being Earthers. Perhaps it was as well we hadn't tried to fight them in Sick Bay. Besides, Michael seemed clumsy still, which was probably the aftereffects of the stun guns; he'd been hit with not only the direct stun at the landing dock, but also the fringe edge of one at the party.

Jamin began to look rebellious as we neared a section that I knew housed only Patrol offices, but the Patrolmen didn't even hesitate there. Having no idea what lay beyond, I was beginning to feel as curious as I was angry. Jamin looked puzzled, and Michael was getting impatient. That made me nervous; there was no telling what he might decide to do. Martians, even though they were the major Colonial participants in the war, never seem to understand how irrationally ruthless Earthers can be. You'd think, having fought that war, they'd know. Maybe they're just too civilized to believe it. I believed it, and I didn't want to die just because Michael was civilized. There had been a chance, very slight, that we could have taken these Patrolmen in Sick Bay, but we certainly couldn't in Patrol territory, where they had ready backup.

I was angling toward Michael in the feeble hope of

staving off any unexpected fits of violence when the Patrolmen jostled us to a halt in the middle of the corridor, and one of them pressed the signal next to a door. It opened onto a control room full of clearly labeled C.I.D. equipment.

"Central Intelligence Division?" Michael's voice was startled.

The Patrolmen waved us into the room. A thin, tidy man with a mustache, who wasn't C.I.D. but could have been a Board Member, noticed us and bounced off a console toward us. "Come in, come in." He sounded positively delighted to see us.

We went in. The door slid shut behind us, with the Patrolmen still outside. "What the hell is this?" asked Michael.

"Space that," I said, but I don't think he heard me.

"Central Intelligence Division?" he said again. Maybe he hoped someone would deny it.

The tidy man looked almost embarrassed. "Well, this is, but I'm not. That is . . ."

Board Advisor Brown appeared suddenly from behind a console. "Skyrider?"

I still didn't understand, but I was glad to see her. "*You* called us here?"

She smiled. "Not exactly."

"What the hell *is* this?" Michael looked perfectly willing to break a few heads over a few C.I.D. consoles if nobody answered him this time.

Board Advisor Brown looked at him curiously. "You must be the Martian who got the tell-tail on board the terrorist ship."

He looked stricken. "They *know* that?"

"Yes. And, as you know, the C.I.D. . . ."

"*Damn* it." He didn't look angry anymore. He

looked sick. "Space the damn C.I.D. *Earthers*." He made that sound like a curse.

A C.I.D. officer, neatly uniformed and clearly labeled like all the consoles, popped out from behind one of them to frown at him. "I warned you, Board Advisor," she said without looking at Board Advisor Brown.

Sometimes I'm slow, but I'm not completely stupid. I had put it together by then: the black object Michael had been carrying, that I had thought was a useless weapon of some sort, had been a tell-tail gun. If he had fired a tell-tail onto the terrorist ship, it could be tracked. The C.I.D. must already know where the hostages were being held.

Where they had been held. No wonder Michael looked sick. Everybody knew what the C.I.D.'s standard response was to hostage situations. "You killed them." I barely recognized my own voice. There wasn't anything nearer to use, so I used Jamin and Michael as surfaces from which to kick into a dive on the C.I.D. officer.

For no other reason than habit, I didn't draw my handgun. There aren't many rules in hand-to-hand combat among Belters, but the use of weapons other than body parts is one so deeply ingrained that I once nearly let a man kill me with a force blade because it didn't occur to me to use my handgun. In personal combat, one doesn't. And I didn't. If I had, I'd probably be dead; the C.I.D.'s weapons are lethal, and the chamber was full of them. That didn't occur to me, either. I was thinking about Collis's brave white face when he carried Michael's son onto the terrorist ship, and asked that hopeful question to help somebody save them.

C.I.D. officers materialized all around us; but since

I hadn't drawn my weapon, and Board Advisor Brown was there to hold them back, and Michael and Jamin were there to pull me off the woman I was trying to shred with my bare hands, I survived the incident with nothing worse than a bruise over my left ear where Jamin was obliged to slug me. "Skyrider," he said. His voice sounded dull and tired, but determined.

Both he and Michael were clinging to me, and somehow we'd got separated from the C.I.D. woman. We'd got rather tangled in the process, and bounced off two walls and a console before we sorted ourselves out. By then I was calm enough to stop fighting, but that was all. I heard someone saying, over and over again, "Oh, damn. Oh, damn," in a thin little voice that I'd never heard before. When I realized it was mine, I shut up.

"They're not dead," said Board Advisor Brown.

At that, all three of us tried to turn to her at once, which only got us tangled up again. *"What?"* Jamin asked my left elbow.

"I said they're not dead," said Board Advisor Brown. "I'm sorry I didn't say so, sooner; I thought you'd realize. . . . I've convinced the C.I.D. not to follow their usual policy in this case."

"Yet," said the woman I'd tried to kill.

I considered trying again, but this wasn't the moment.

Board Advisor Brown looked at me. "Skyrider, will you people sort yourselves out and talk sense?" she asked impatiently. "I'd like you to meet, um, McCormick." She looked sheepish and maybe embarrassed; one of her best traits, in my opinion, was that she couldn't lie worth a damn. Goodness only knew why "McCormick" thought she had to keep her real name a secret from the three of us: spies will be spies, I suppose. "McCormick," said Board Advisor Brown, "this is the Skyrider, her wingmate Jamin, and, oh, I'm sorry, I don't know your name."

"Michael Rendell," said Michael. He sounded dazed. "They're not dead yet? C.I.D. knows where they are, and they're not dead?"

"Yet," said McCormick. The other C.I.D. officers, seeing I let that go by without attacking her again, began to fade back in amongst the consoles. "As you know, the C.I.D. does not treat with terrorists."

"You'd rather just kill them, and hostages with them," I said.

She lifted an elegant eyebrow at me. "Do you realize that this is the first hostage situation that has arisen since we instituted that policy and proved we meant it?"

"How many civilians did you kill, proving it?"

She pursed her lips. "I don't quite know. Nor do I know the exact number of hostages killed by terrorists or by official rescue efforts before we established the practice. I do know that no more hostages will be taken when people are convinced it will avail them nothing but, perhaps, a quicker death."

"Hostages were taken today," I said.

If I thought the reminder would bother her, I was wrong. She smiled. It was a happy smile. With her sweet, dark, round face and her big, innocent, limpid eyes, she looked like she'd just got an invitation to a particularly delightful party. "That's true. I mentioned that this is the first hostage situation since we established our policy. Actually, a demonstration at this time couldn't be more useful. It would prove we haven't—"

I didn't hear the rest of what she had to say: I was

busy trying to get free of Michael and Jamin so I could rearrange her happy, innocent face. Since it was their kids she was talking about demonstrating on, not mine, that might seem a trifle strange to someone who didn't know the three of us. The plain fact is, Michael and Jamin both had at least a modicum of good sense. I've never been accused of that in my life. At least, not often.

But it wasn't Jamin or Michael who stopped me, really; it was Board Advisor Brown. She said, "Skyrider, for goodness' sake, stop showing off. Stop that, I said. Will you please just calm down long enough to listen to me for a moment? I want you to go after the hostages."

CHAPTER FIVE

The hostages had been taken to Station Newhome, an ancient freefall station built in the days when the only way to create artificial gravity was to give a station adequate spin and then fight the effects of Coriolis force. Newhome didn't have that spin. Old as it was, it had been in use right up till the Colonial Incident, when it had been the scene of one of the longest and bitterest sieges of the war. The Colonials didn't give up. Their bodies were taken off the station shortly after the war, and as far as I knew, that was the last anyone had anything to do with Station Newhome till now.

The little man with the mustache, whose name turned out to be Starkey and whose job title was never mentioned, assured us that Newhome was in good repair. "Once the tell-tail had led us there, I was able to study it with these extremely long-range scanners. There's evidence of quite a lot of activity in and around the station. See, here, on the flight deck?'' He pointed to a meaningless pattern of lines on one of his screens. "These are shuttles, do you see them? Starbirds, at a guess, with maybe a few Falcons, or even Fords, I'm afraid it's a bit difficult at this range. . . ."

"You can't make it, of course," said McCormick. She smiled quite pleasantly as she said it. "That station was well built, and is easily defensible, as Earth learned during the Insurrection. You can't get them out of there alive. At best, you'll just be killing yourselves, and we'll still have to blast the station."

"Thanks for the vote of confidence," I said. "If the station is so easy to blast, why didn't you do it during the war?"

"I couldn't get authorization, then."

"Ah. But you think you can, now."

Starkey continued his demonstration as if we hadn't spoken. "I have the plans for Newhome right here somewhere." He said it with the anxious excitement of an absent-minded scientist on the verge of an important discovery. "Really, wait a moment, I just have to find the right code."

"I know the layout," said Michael. "I've been there."

McCormick lifted an eyebrow at him. "When?"

He permitted himself a tense little smile. "During the war." He didn't elaborate, and she didn't have time to question him further; from across the chamber someone said, "Message coming in," and she gave us an agitated glance and kicked away from us to see what the message was.

"Here they are," said Starkey, and I turned back to his screens. More lines: but these, at least, were in a recognizable pattern. It was essentially a blueprint of the whole station, flashing by in stages across one screen. He pointed. "They repaired this section just before the Insurrection, see the changes? And here's where they took out the old generators, to put in the malite converters, I forget just when that was, it should be dated here, let's see, but I guess that isn't important. These curving lines are the maintenance tubes. And this is the flight deck, but I suppose that will be too heavily guarded to be of use to you." He drew back from the screen, frowning. "Actually, I don't quite see how you will get past them at all. There was a shuttle dock put in here, around the turn of the century, probably about the same time they updated the flight deck and removed the bay doors, but it will be abandoned now; there's no activity in this whole section of the station as far as I can tell; and even if it were still in use, that is, if it has a working synch system, well, you can see you'd need their cooperation to dock there, you won't have access to the synch system, otherwise."

"The Skyrider doesn't need synch systems." Jamin gave me an odd little grin I couldn't quite interpret.

"No?" Starkey asked dubiously, and looked distractedly back at the screen. "Well. Yes. I suppose an expert and, you'll forgive me, perhaps crazy pilot *could* attempt a dead-dock here."

"She dead-docked with the *Marabou*," said Board Advisor Brown. "Would this be more difficult?"

"Oh, my, yes," said Starkey; and then, "Well . . . No, er, I don't quite know, actually, I suppose not. . . . With the *Marabou*?" He looked at me. "You dead-docked with the *Marabou*? That was you? But the *Marabou* was crippled in flight, I hardly thought, I mean, I give little credence to rumors, as a rule, you mean you actually did dead-dock with her? But surely . . . ?"

McCormick floated gently back to us. "That was the terrorists."

Starkey looked at her uncertainly. "What was?"

"They identified themselves. Colonials, as I suspected."

None of us bothered to argue with her; it wasn't the time.

"They gave us a list of political prisoners they want released." When she said "political prisoners" she used a tone that made it sound like it meant rockdust, or maybe worse refuse; certainly not people. "They found your tell-tail, Martian, so they know we know where they are. Since we know, and we haven't yet blasted them, they naturally assume they're going to get away with this. Now they've started asking for the repeal of whatever laws they don't happen to like."

"What laws?" I didn't really suppose she'd answer, but I was curious.

She made a negligent gesture that nearly dislodged her from the freefall handhold through which she'd hooked one arm. "Just laws. Whatever occurs to them, I suppose. Property ownership; that sort of thing."

"Absurd requests like maybe that Fallers should be allowed to own real estate?" Jamin's tone was dangerous, though his expression gave nothing away.

McCormick just nodded. "That sort of thing." She looked mildly irritated. "If we had blasted them—"

"May I remind you," said Board Advisor Brown, with a quelling glance at me in case I got an urge to show off some more on McCormick's pretty face, "that the request *not* to blast Station Newhome came directly from the President herself?"

"We have jurisdiction here," said McCormick. "The President . . ."

"Has very little control over her 'universal peace-keeping agency,' " I said. "Yes. We know. Thank the gods whatever control she has, has held this long. Starkey, show me that section with the abandoned shuttle dock again."

"If you can dock," said Michael, "I know the layout of the station."

"I work alone," I said.

"Rockdust," said Jamin.

"A small force, led by an expert pilot, just might have a chance," said Starkey. "With complete knowledge of the station's layout, you could conceivably penetrate it successfully. The area around the shuttle dock, here, you see it on the screen? This is deserted, and over here, look, it's a different level, let's see, yes, here, I'd guess the hostages would be held in this area, it's not far from the flight deck or the central control area, most of the station will probably be deserted unless this terrorist force is much larger than we've been led to believe, although of course that, too, is possible, considering the number of shuttles on the flight deck, but I really don't quite see—"

"Starkey," said Board Advisor Brown.

He looked up, his clear brown eyes vaguely interested. "Yes?"

"Can you transfer that information to the Skyrider's computer?"

"The Skyrider?" His attention was all on his screens again. "What computer?"

"The one on the *Defiance*," I said. He looked up at me distractedly, and I added, "That's my ship. A Falcon. She's on the flight deck here. I can access her computer from your console, and you could feed

in everything you have on Station Newhome. Then
we could study it to our hearts' content on our way
out to Newhome.''

''You'll be going, then?'' He seemed surprised.

''That's what this meeting is all about, isn't it?''

He frowned thoughtfully. ''Why, yes, I suppose it
is.''

McCormick had a few more choice opinions to
offer on the topic of chasing terrorists, but none of
them seemed to me to be germane. We accessed the
Defiance computer, fed it what Starkey had on Station Newhome, and had another argument about how
many of us would go. Of course I knew I couldn't
keep Jamin or Michael from coming along with me.
In all likelihood I'd be glad of it before we were
done. But the argument did serve a purpose. It kept
McCormick from insisting on sending along any C.I.D.
people. If I objected that strenuously to being accom-
panied by my friends, I just might abandon the whole
endeavor if she tried to supply me with members of a
group we all knew would never qualify as my friends.
And despite her bravado about jurisdiction and the
President's influence, I thought she'd have a little
trouble earning her next promotion if the rescue mission didn't take off and the President learned it was
McCormick who stopped it.

Once we had the Station Newhome data in my
computer, there should have been nothing further to
keep us from leaving. McCormick still didn't like it,
but I thought she'd let us go without any more nonsense. I've always been an optimist. She slipped
away somewhere while Starkey and I were feeding
my computer, and when she came back she handed
Board Advisor Brown a message that made Brown
stare and think about cursing. Instead, she pressed

her lips together in a thin, straight line, and looked at me. "You're ready to go?"

McCormick made a startled little movement beside her, but didn't say anything; when I looked at her, her face was almost expressionless. Only the faintest gleam of malice showed in her eyes. I looked back at Board Advisor Brown and nodded. "We're ready."

Brown looked thoughtful for a moment, then resigned. "Good. I'm afraid there'll be a brief delay, but we'll get you off as quickly as possible."

This time it was Jamin who made a startled movement, but he didn't say anything, and he was as good as McCormick at keeping his face expressionless. In the Belt, he might have tried something; but here, we were too near Earth and surrounded by Earthers.

Michael, who was a Grounder and therefore generally agreed to be human even though he chose to live on Mars, was more accustomed to standing up for his rights. Which was reasonable; being fully human, he had more rights to stand up for, even to Earthers. He looked from Brown to McCormick and back again, and I couldn't read the expression on his boyish, freckled face: I thought for a moment he was just deciding which of them to hit. But he didn't make a move. He just asked, in the calm, quiet voice of one who was accustomed to having his questions answered, what would cause the delay.

Brown wasn't a Board Advisor for nothing. Giving Michael a quick, reassuring smile, she turned gracefully toward the door and said calmly, as if it were a matter of complete indifference, "I'll tell you about it as we go along; that will save time."

We had followed her obediently into the corridor before I fully realized how neatly we'd been maneuvered away from McCormick. I paused and glanced back at the door as it slid shut behind us. "You're pretty damn loose, aren't you?" I said.

She smiled absently. "If that means I just manipulated your reactions rather neatly, I guess I am." She was propelling herself along the corridor, and we had to follow if we wanted to hear what she said. "I couldn't let any of you tangle with that woman," she said, with a glance at Michael that was both friendly and shy. "She's too dangerous, and I don't mean just as an opponent in a brawl."

"What made you think we'd try to tangle with her?"

"The delay I mentioned is a briefing she set up."

"A briefing?"

We were negotiating a corner, and her face was turned away from me. "The VIPs whose families were taken hostage want to see who's going after them, and make sure you're fully equipped and advised for the mission."

"Rockdust. What for?"

"And how'd they know anyone was going after them?" asked Michael. In freefall, one didn't usually notice how large he was; height didn't matter there, and his bulk was entirely in proportion to his height. Now, however, still rankled by McCormick's behavior, he looked dangerous—and quite large.

Jamin just looked lean and resigned. "McCormick told them, how else? But, space, why would they want to delay us, when the alternative to us, for the hostages, is death by C.I.D.?"

"Even if we're totally incompetent," I said, "and even if these people can determine that by meeting us, what have they got to lose by letting us go? All we're risking is our lives. The hostages' lives are already forfeit, surely?"

"They don't want to delay you," said Board Advisor Brown. She sounded very calm and reasonable, and I still couldn't see her face. "Once they learned you were going, they probably had a perfectly natural desire to see you. Possibly even to thank you in advance for risking your lives; they won't expect to have the opportunity later, since as far as anyone can tell who doesn't know what you can do, this is a ridiculous proposition with very little, if any, chance of success."

"The chance gets smaller, the longer we delay," I said.

She glanced back at me, and I saw that her face was as calm as her voice. Well, they weren't her hostages. "You know that. I know that. Because we know there really is a chance. These people are grasping at straws, and they don't expect straws to sustain them, or whatever it is straws are supposed to do for people who grasp them. Also, don't forget the bureaucratic mind. These are bureaucrats. They don't recognize delay as a hazard, in any situation."

"Okay, fine, they don't think they're jeopardizing the mission by putting eyetracks all over us before we go, I'll accept that, but why didn't someone *tell* them? McCormick set this up, you say. She's no bureaucrat. She knows what a delay could cost us."

Brown gave me an odd little smile. "She wanted to make a demonstration, or had you forgotten?"

"I guess I'd forgotten she's an Earther. Their brutality startles me, sometimes. Only an Earther—"

"I'm an Earther," said Board Advisor Brown.

"Oh. Sorry. I know you are."

"I didn't say that just to embarrass you, Skyrider. I said it to remind you. If everyone could only understand that people aren't labels, and that labels aren't people . . . Well, never mind. Here we are.'' She pushed the signal beside a door and we watched it slide open beneath us.

The chamber beyond had been designed for Earthers. It had Terran furniture bolted to one of the walls: a great wooden table and matching chairs, with fabrics covering the chairbacks and even the seats, and with gravity trays at regular intervals along the table top so drinks could be placed there without floating away. On the walls that hadn't been selected to serve as floor or ceiling, there were holograms of Earth scenes: a sunlit forest; a city street, with moving cars and pedestrians; and a group of children playing in a park.

Most of the people waiting to meet us were Earthers; nobody else would strap himself primly into a seat at a table bolted to an arbitrarily selected wall in a freefall station. There were a few Martians hanging uncertainly next to unoccupied chairs, and several Belters floating carelessly wherever air currents and their own small movements took them. At first glance, they seemed to have very little in common except that they all looked important, with that unconscious arrogance people have who are accustomed to power; and they all looked scared.

CHAPTER SIX

Board Advisor Brown introduced us to the assembly, but didn't bother introducing the members of the assembly to us; she knew we hadn't the patience for any polite formalities that could be avoided. She also saved us some time by telling them our general qualifications before they could ask: I was the expert and crazy pilot who could perform the dead-dock, as I had recently proved with the *Marabou*; Michael had been a Colonial Warrior on Station Newhome, and was familiar with its layout; and Jamin was the only backup pilot I would permit to fly my Falcon, and a good infighter experienced in freefall combat as well.

They listened in relative silence. I have seldom been so solemnly judged by so many anxious eyes. When she concluded by saying that the sooner we got started the better, and that delay could mean the failure of our mission before we even got started, nobody took offense. They were probably all too busy worrying to notice.

Nobody said anything right away when she had finished. She kicked off gently from the doorway to float serenely to an empty chair at the head of the table, caught hold of its back to steady herself, and floated there, watching them. Michael, like most people who spend the major portion of their lives in gravity of one kind or another, wanted something to anchor him from random movement in freefall: he looked around, apparently decided a place at the table would make him a little too cozy with the VIPs, and settled for hooking his ankle onto a freefall handhold next to the door. Jamin and I just relaxed where we were, and waited.

A severely dressed woman at the far end of the table made a sudden movement. "What can you hope to accomplish?" Her eyes were dark and bitter. "What are you planning?"

I hesitated. Michael said quietly, "We plan to rescue the hostages."

Her bitter eyes examined him sharply. "How?"

"We don't know yet, exactly," I said. "We'll study the station's layout on our way out to it, and we'll formulate a plan, as well as we can, then."

Across the table from the bitter woman, a sleek blond man made a sound of disapproval. "As well as you can!"

A Belter, floating over their heads, unfolded his long legs so he could kick at a wall, getting himself down to their level. "I've had some dealings with this kind of strike force action." His bushy white eyebrows shaded his eyes, making him look at once genial and mildly dangerous. "And I'm familiar, as I think we all are, with the Skyrider's record. I know it sounds irresponsible for them to set out without a clear plan, but believe me, it's not uncommon."

Another Earther shifted against the straps that held his considerable bulk to a seat. "Not uncommon. What does that mean, exactly?"

The Belter turned his way, his expression startlingly civil. "Nothing in itself, of course, Gen; except that it can be done, and has been done, by others equally competent."

Gen gave him a puzzled, distant smile, not at all friendly, but not really unfriendly, either. "It can be done." He sounded thoughtful. "Yes, of course. But . . . successfully?"

"Look, folks." They all turned to look at me in surprise; it was probably quite unorthodox for me to speak up while they were engaged in their polite discussion, but I've never been much good at waiting. "I don't like to interfere with your accustomed processes, but we are in something of a hurry, as Board Advisor Brown mentioned: the longer we take getting out to Station Newhome, the more time the terrorists have to figure out that we're coming, and get ready to fight us off. So I'm going to put it to you simply. Bluntly, maybe. If you think I'm being rude, I'm sorry. I'm trying to save some lives. Including my own."

Most of them looked at least moderately interested.

"The thing of it is, the only risk involved here is the lives of me and my friends. Just Michael and Jamin and me. That's all."

"But, my wife, my son," said a Martian, floating agitatedly away from the chair to which he'd been anchored.

"If the terrorists have your wife and your son," I said, "their lives are already forfeit. I'm sorry, but that's how it is. We don't even know whether they're still alive, right now. We do know what the C.I.D. would like to do to them.''

"Well, really," said a plump Earther woman with diamonds in her hair.

"Yes, really," I said. "We've just come from the C.I.D. They're vexed that they haven't been allowed to blast Station Newhome out of space already. If Michael and Jamin and I fail, that's just what they'll do: blast it, with hostages and terrorists all on board. But if we don't go, that's still what they'll do. It's their standard policy in what they call a hostage situation, we all know that. And if it comes right down to it, the policy is brutal, and repugnant, and I don't like it one bit, but it does work. It works, and has worked, for years now. Think how many so-called hostage situations there used to be, before the C.I.D. got tough. Think how many have occurred since. None, till now, right? So the policy works, and I'm not really arguing against it in general. But this time, because there's a chance of success, I want to try something else first, before the C.I.D. has its way. What I'm trying to say is, it's the *only* chance those hostages have: if we don't go, they die; if we go, and fail, they die; but if we go, and succeed, they live. It's as simple as that. I know I haven't put it well. I'm not a diplomat. But please, try to see past the presentation to the facts.''

A Martian smiled, suddenly. It was a dull, tired smile, but it was a smile. "No," he said, "you're not a diplomat. But the facts are there, and we do have to face them.''

"Well, really," said the plump Earther with diamonds.

"People, please," said Board Advisor Brown. They all turned to her, in one unified movement, full of

hope. Maybe they thought she would produce some
unexpected possibility, like a rabbit out of a hat. But
they already had all the possibilities they were going
to get on this one. "The Skyrider said it," she said.
"The only chance the hostages have is these three
people. And the hope gets smaller, the longer we
keep them here. So instead of impeding them with
our questions and doubts and fears, I suggest we
concentrate on helping them prepare, and getting
them off on their mission just as quickly as we can
manage. Now. Has anyone any suggestions as to how
we can help insure the success of the mission?"

"But we don't know the plan," said a Martian.

"There isn't any plan," said Brown.

"You know all the plan there is," said Michael,
with deliberate patience. "We've put all the Newhome
data in the Skyrider's ship's computer. We'll study it
on our way. We know there's an abandoned shuttle
dock, and the Skyrider thinks she can dead-dock
there. What happens once we're inside will depend
on how accurate our information is, and on whether
we can evade the terrorists long enough to get the
hostages free. Those are things we can't plan for,
from here."

"You could carry personal Comm Links," said a
Belter.

"In case they get separated," said an Earther.

"And to keep them apprised of what's going on
outside," said the Belter.

"Couldn't they have the terrorist frequency?" asked
a Martian. "Do we know what it is? That would
surely help."

"Good idea," said a Belter. "And what about
weapons?"

"We have our side arms," I said into the embarrassed silence that question produced.

"We can't really provide anything better than what they've got," said the diamonded Earther.

"Of course not," said a round, angry Belter. "It would be against the law."

"Oh, don't fuss," said a Martian. "What about this shuttle of yours, Skyrider? You don't have weapons there, of course. But . . . I understand some of the Belt shuttles do carry lasers, in case of bad rock flurries?"

"I have lasers," I said. "And photars."

That caused a rustle among the Earthers, quickly controlled as they realized that, however quasi-legal my weaponry was, it was in their best interest at this time not to start quoting regulations at me.

A little black man with gentle eyes, in the uniform of the defeated Martian Army, straightened abruptly beside his chair. "That's it, then. I assume you don't want any backup shuttles, or that sort of thing?" When I shook my head, he continued, "This type of exercise is not wholly unfamiliar to me. And it occurs to me, neither is it wholly unfamiliar to the C.I.D. I'm afraid we've been convened primarily to create an obstacle in your path; and while I am shocked at such behavior on the part of the C.I.D. or its officers, this is not the time to discuss such matters. Do you, Skyrider, see any means whereby we can be of further use to you?"

"Not except by letting us go."

He nodded again, with obvious satisfaction. "A direct question, and a direct answer. I admire your courage, all three of you." He looked around the table, at the puzzled and anxious faces all turned, now, to him. "I suggest we continue this discussion *after* the mission is under way."

"You mean, send them off? Now?" asked a pink Martian.

The Martian Army officer nodded. "Exactly. If no one has any cogent objections? No? Then go, with our blessing," he told me. "We will see to it that your personal Comm Links are delivered to your shuttle at once. May all the gods go with you."

I wasn't sure about the gods, but the personal Comms went with us. As promised, they were waiting on the flight deck when we got there. Since I had, out of habit, locked the *Defiance* against all entry, the Comms had been left on a gravity tray beside the forward hatch. There was a note beside them, sent by Board Advisor Brown. It said, "I thought you didn't volunteer for suicide missions. Did you forget to ask for pay?"

I looked at it for a second, wiped the message, and printed out simply, "I didn't forget." Let her figure it out. I sent the message unit on its way back to her and unlocked the hatch to let us onto the *Defiance*.

"What was that about?" asked Michael.

"Welcome aboard the *Defiance*," I said.

He looked at me quizzically and floated on past, through the hatch. As far as anyone could tell without a very careful, thorough inspection, she was a standard issue Falcon, with no apparent alterations, except the lasers and photars, since she came out of the factory. I wasn't interested in interior decoration, and hadn't modified her standard fittings in any way. The cockpit had two control seats, the usual banks of control panels, and standard scanner screens. Earthers usually covered non-critical surfaces with fabrics and furs; Martians, with their mania for technological toys, often added extra scanners of various types, computer printout and message consoles in addition to those supplied by the factory, and various odds and ends to do with interior environment control and creature comforts; and I'd seen Belter shuttles stripped clean of absolutely everything that wasn't directly essential to operation. I'd done none of that, so there wasn't much of anything that Michael, who had never been on board before, could comment on, unless he wanted to comment on the lack of modification.

He didn't. An Earther might have; they seem to need to say something in almost any situation, no matter how meaningless or even offensive speech may be. Martians, like Belters, are more taciturn. An Earther would call it less polite. Michael just looked around the cockpit, nodded once, and got out of the way while Jamin and I took the control seats.

I punched in for clearance, got it, and lifted off. There was a lot of activity on the flight deck; several Patrol shuttles coming and going, and a lot of work-people gathered around some stationary shuttles on the other side of the deck. None of them were in my way, so I ignored them.

"C.I.D. wouldn't send out the Patrol without the President's approval, would they?" asked Michael.

We cleared the deck, popping gently through the force screen into space, and had to dodge a cluster of Patrol Starbirds taking up a recon formation just outside. "They'd damn well better not, if they're fond of living," I said crossly.

"They may not be aware of the hazard." He was behind me, so I couldn't see his face, but his tone was gently amused, which I found irritating.

"Jamin keeps telling me my reputation precedes me."

"And he's right, but maybe not everyone believes it."

"That's their problem." I hit the thrusters to take us away from there with all due haste. "You're quiet, Jamin. We've been in worse fixes than this. What is it?"

He just looked at me.

"We will get him back, you know."

"You keep saying that."

"Only because it's true."

"I shouldn't have let them take him in the first place."

"What should you have done, knocked out the lot of them on the spot? I seem to recall that you tried. It was a damnfool thing to do, and I don't see how you could have done more."

He shook his head. "I don't know. He's just a boy."

"Is that what's bothering you? Listen, that's a Belter kid you're raising." I told him about the scene at the shuttle dock. "So don't worry about his youthful sensitivities; Collis is all right. Hell, by the time we get there, he may have engineered an escape for the whole lot of them."

He tried a grin, but it wasn't very successful. "A month ago, I'd have said you talk like that because you just don't give a damn."

I shrugged, which can be hazardous in freefall, but I was strapped to my seat, so it didn't matter. "Come to that, I don't give a damn."

"Oh, no. You've really blown it, this time, you know. You didn't strike any kind of bargain for pay; you just started after them." He gave me the same odd little grin he'd given me in the C.I.D. chamber, when he said I didn't need synch systems; and I still couldn't quite interpret it. There was sympathy in it, and surpɹise, and something else. "I thought you didn't volunteer for suicide missions," he said.

"That's exactly what Board Advisor Brown said. I wondered at the time whether you'd been talking to her, or something. She wondered whether I'd forgot to ask for pay."

"When did she say all that?" He wasn't really interested, but talking about anything helped keep his mind off Collis.

"That was the message she left with our Comm Links."

"Yes? What did you answer?"

"Just that I hadn't forgot."

"I didn't hear you bargaining."

"Of course not. I'll extract my payment later. Listen, I'm no fool. You saw those VIPs at the meeting. They all think we're just generously throwing away our lives on some sort of heroic gesture for the sake of the thing. Right? Well, wrong. I ain't throwing away my life for the sake of anything. I *like* my life. But what kind of bargain could I have struck with them, then? Maybe they'd have come through, but it would have delayed things, and they might just have decided to stop us because our motives weren't pure enough. If they decided we weren't making a grand gesture, they might have thought we were playing some kind of trick on them. They're politicians, and that's what politicians do, and it's what they expect everyone else to do. They'd at least have been after me to tell them what my game was."

"When all along, your game was to convince them you're making a grand gesture?" asked Michael.

"Just so," I said. "And when it succeeds, what wouldn't they grant the returning hero? They'll give me the Earth if I ask for it."

"What would you want with it?" asked Jamin.

"Well, maybe not the Earth," I said thoughtfully. "But we could use a Falcon with your name on it. The *Defiance* gets just a little crowded sometimes. Like when you get all self-righteous about my mercenary tendencies."

"If we pull this off," he said, "you can hand them as big a bill as you like for your services, and I promise I won't say a word against mercenaries."

"I'll hold you to that."

"You believe this rockdust?" Michael asked him. "You honestly think Melacha is doing this only for personal gain?"

"Shut up," I explained.

CHAPTER SEVEN

We had plenty of time to study the Newhome data on our way out to its orbit. Between the computer tapes and Michael's memory, we had information on every square centimeter of the station, including the control systems, storage, and dead areas. But we never did formulate a plan. We chose the three most likely places in which to find the hostages, drew lots to see which of us would investigate which area, and that was the extent of it. We discussed a lot of possibilities as to what we'd do if this or that thing happened, but made no decision that the crowd of VIPs we'd left behind would have regarded as a plan.

The things that concerned us most were the things we didn't talk about. We went to great lengths to avoid speculation on the current condition of the hostages. There was no way to know whether they were alive or dead; whether, if they were alive, they were well or ill treated; whether they had given in to fear and despair or managed, somehow, to hold out some illogical hope of rescue. I spent a lot of time trying not to remember the pinched white look on Collis's face when he entered the terrorist ship. The memory shook me more than I'd have cared to admit. I preferred to think of him, when I thought of him at all, giggling and bouncing off the walls as he had been before the party. To think how frightened he must be was heart-wrenching.

That in itself unnerved me. The hotshot image I maintained, of the careless and carefree Skyrider, the loner who didn't and wouldn't give a floating damn for anybody in space but herself, who would gamble with destruction any time on a whim, but who wouldn't go one kilometer out of her way for anybody else's sake, was something I had built with great care, for a reason. It wasn't a reason I had ever thought out to myself in words, any more than it was an image I really believed in completely. But I wanted to believe it. Maybe I needed to believe it. Never mind what I actually *did*: I wanted to *feel* that I was free to cut my losses and run, any time I got an urge to do so.

I couldn't run from Collis. And I didn't like knowing it. It wasn't a comfortable piece of self-knowledge. It was scary. If one little kid, with his flashing smile and his trusting eyes, could hook me into a suicide mission like this without even remembering to demand proper payment before I set out, what the hell was happening to my life? What the hell was happening to *me?*

Michael and Jamin were just as eager as I to avoid all mention of the hostages, though presumably for different reasons. I caught each of them, more than once on that trip, floating absently beside some task half-finished, his expression distant, his eyes bleak, his face drawn with worry. I don't think they ever caught me looking like that, but I couldn't swear to it. If either of them did, at least he was polite enough not to mention it.

We saw a lot of Patrol activity in the regions between the station we'd left behind and the one we were headed for, but though we listened to every news broadcast we could find, and even managed to hook into the Patrol frequency a couple of times, we couldn't find out what they were doing. There was a lot of flight activity in general: Starbirds, Falcons, some old Fords and Chevys, and even a few of the new Sunfinches showed on our scanners from time to time. As far as I knew, nobody but Company high muckymucks and government agencies flew Sunfinches. Only one of those crossed our path near enough for hailing; and its only response to our signal was a sudden dive off our scanner screens, so neat and quick it left me blinking. Which proved the government really had come up with a new malite conversion drive every bit as good as rumors had suggested. But it didn't tell me what the Sunfinch had been doing out there in the first place.

We got some odd Comm Link pickups from the direction of Mars, as well. The messages were in code, and too brief to trace with any certainty, but we knew what they were about. There was an army assembling out there. Maybe the whole supposedly vanquished Colonial Fleet.

"I wonder if those terrorists have any idea what they might have started?" Michael asked after we'd heard one of those ambiguous, staticky Martian messages. "This could turn into the first battle in another goddamned war."

"Of course they know," I said impatiently. "Earth has been trying to push us back into war for a long

time now. She knows the Colonies are gearing up for
it.''

"But we aren't ready. And we'd as soon avoid it,
really, anyway." He looked puzzled. "Those terrorists are Colonials. They must know we're not ready."

"You think they're Colonials? You're as bad as an
Earther. Why do you think they're Colonials? Just
because some of them were wearing cast-off Colonial
clothes?"

He looked at me. We were in the galley, going
over the Newhome plans again with our lunch, and
listening to the Comm Link. He'd spent too many
years in gravity; he kept trying to put things down.
Now he placed his sandwich carefully on the galley
table, and didn't notice when it started to float apart.
"You think they were Earthers?"

I caught a piece of his sandwich and handed it to
him. "Hang onto that, or we'll be picking it out of
the air filters forever. Of course they were Earthers.
You saw how they moved in freefall, you heard them
talking, and you saw what they did. How they just
shot anybody at random. You think a Colonial could
have done that?"

"Well, no, not as a rule, but, space, Melacha,
terrorists aren't rational people. You can't expect
them to behave by rational rules." He caught the rest
of his sandwich and held it, looking young and ear-
nest and rather troubled.

"I'm not talking about rules," I said. "I'm talking
about, I don't know, something more like instinct, I
suppose. I mean, it's like how you just put your
sandwich on the table, unconsciously relying on gravity to hold it there; in gravity, I've seen Jamin carefully place something in the air beside him and look
surprised when it falls. Those aren't good examples,

because you could just say they're habit, but in a way, what I'm talking about is sort of a habit of thinking.

"I know there are aberrant Colonials, same like there are aberrant anybodies, but a whole group of them so aberrant that they could totally ignore the Colonial regard for individual lives? Particularly the lives of children? We're almost pathological about it. We live hard, we play rough, we fight over what's for breakfast, but we *don't* spray-stun clusters of innocent bystanders, and we absolutely do *not* risk the lives of children. Children are sacred. They are our future. They're our lives, our hopes, our proof that what we're doing can be done: that Humankind doesn't have to root around on Earth like a bunch of grubby animals forever; that we can have the freedom of the whole Solar System, and a new generation ready to take over where we leave off. You think a Colonial, any real Colonial, could break that conditioning enough to not just take children as hostages, which is bad enough, but even to stun a few of them into the bargain?"

He said doubtfully, "Anybody can go crazy."

"Sure, all right, but a group of crazies, all crazy in the same unlikely way?"

He examined his sandwich thoughtfully. There were shadows in his eyes: shadows that had never really faded since the war that put them there. "Of course you're right," he said. "But if I didn't see that, and I'm a Colonial myself . . ."

"I know. We'll never convince the Earthers. It's just like the *Marabou* thing all over again. Neat as neat. Nasty Colonials playing rough against innocent Earthers. Did you notice that most of the hostages were Earthers? I know we're not yet ready for war. I hope to hell we don't even want one. But we may just have one now, ready or not."

The Comm Link cracked static on the Martian frequency, and said in a distant, small voice, "Red Leader."

After a pause, another voice said, "Blue box."

More static. Silence. Then: "Understood."

"That's another squadron," said Michael. "I wish we knew what the Earther forces are doing."

"Assembling to ward off the Colonial Fleet, I expect."

"We need that new conversion drive," he said.

"Like the Sunfinches have?"

He nodded. "I'd heard it was good, but I wouldn't have believed how good if we hadn't seen it in action. That thing went so fast the whole rest of the universe might as well have been standing still."

"Relatively speaking, I suppose we were."

"It's no joke, damn it."

"I know. Without it, I suppose, if they push us into war now, we don't have much of a chance."

"If they've got something that much better than anything we have, we don't have any chance. Not one chance in hell. They've got all the manpower, the resources, the force of law, and a power base I don't even like to think about. And if they have their way, they'll have the public image, too; we'll be the dreadful aggressors." He finished his sandwich and carefully chased all the crumbs he could catch into the nearest disposal.

"And if we had a Sunfinch?"

He gave me a tight little grin. "Then we'd have *one* chance in hell. Which doesn't sound like much; but, given a little time to get into production, we could sure as space turn it into something."

"You make it sound like getting a Sunfinch is really our only chance, if it comes to war."

"I think it is. Particularly if we lose public sympathy."

I finished my own sandwich, and joined him in crumb-chasing. "Then we'll just have to get a Sunfinch, won't we?"

He probably would have berated me again for joking about serious matters, if Jamin hadn't called us just then on the intercom to let us know he had Station Newhome on the scanners. We left the rest of the sandwich crumbs for the air filter to take care of, and propelled ourselves out of the galley toward the cockpit.

When we got there, Jamin had Newhome on the main screen, where we could all see it. We were still far enough from it that it was only a brighter daub of light against a background of unblinking stars; but at maximum magnification it soon resolved into a weird, abstract cluster of oddly shaped units joined at unexpected angles, like a pile of geometrically cut and trimmed rocks drawn loosely together by the gravity of their mass.

Our flight path had taken us past Newhome's orbit and back in toward it on what the blueprints said should be a blind side. The flight deck and control area were out of our sight on the other side of the cluster; on this side, on one of the nearer units, we should find the abandoned shuttle dock we hoped to use. I took the control seat next to Jamin's and strapped in. Michael hovered between us, studying the screens.

"The shuttle dock is on Unit Seven," he said. "That spherical one on the left side of the screen."

I kept the whole mass on the screen while I jockeyed in as fast as I safely could; the nearer we were, the less chance we stood of getting caught in the terrorists' scanners. When we were near enough, I narrowed the view to Unit Seven, and got the shuttle dock on the screen. It looked undamaged, so far.

This was where the "expert pilot" business would come in; the shuttle dock was designed for use with a synch system, whereby my shuttle's computer and one on Station Newhome would operate in tandem to precisely synchronize the speed and rotation of the *Defiance* to that of Station Newhome. Without Newhome's cooperation, I would have to perform that exacting task manually. Matching orbital speed wasn't too difficult, but managing at the same time to exactly duplicate the station's axial rotation with a much smaller shuttle wasn't so simple. And if I didn't get it absolutely right, we'd end up squashed across the side of Unit Seven like rockdust on a viewscreen.

I once likened landing on a flight deck to landing on one blade of a spinning fan (axial rotation) while the fan moves toward one or away at considerable speed (orbital velocity). This was even more difficult, because I didn't have a whole flight deck to play with. I had to hit the shuttle dock exactly; and the smallest error, even if it didn't kill us, could cause us to shear off the docking hooks and prevent a successful connection.

I'd done it on the *Marabou*; and, before that, a lot of times on Rat Johnson's rock. I suppose it did get a bit easier after all that practice, but it certainly hadn't gotten any less scary. I've never made a dead-dock yet that I really expected to live through. I don't suppose I ever will. Maybe that's part of why I do it: that old, heart-shaking, breath-taking, dizzy-making thrill at the edge of death.

My sweet *Defiance* responded to my commands almost before I made them. She was an extension of my body, reaching gently, gently, for that shuttle dock, with movements as precise and delicate and neat as a freefall dancer's. Out of the corner of my eye I saw Michael gripping the backs of both control seats, so hard his knuckles turned white. Beside me, Jamin, who had watched me do the same thing when we caught the *Marabou*, almost managed to look confident, but not quite. I grinned. "Such a touching display of faith in me," I said. "Hang on, doubters. We're going in." We went.

CHAPTER EIGHT

It wasn't the best docking anybody ever did, but it wasn't bad, either. My aim was only off by a couple of millimeters. Since I had the speeds right, that only meant we hung there for a paralyzing second before the docking mechanisms slid home and I hit the switch for the hooks. As soon as they were securely engaged, I cut the engines, and we sat there in silence while the men slowly relaxed. I needed the time, too, having got a little bit tense myself in that uncertain second, but I didn't see any reason to mention that.

Jamin was the first of us to finally make a move. He got the personal Comms out of the equipment case where we'd stashed them, handed one to each of us, and put on his own. They were clever little devices that fit over one ear. We had three settings on ours: one for the terrorist frequency, one for public news reports, and one for communication between ourselves. A light tap on the main body of the thing, a button behind the ear, changed the frequency sequentially. They were set now on public news. One tap would switch them to the terrorist frequency, another would change them to intercom, and a third would move them back to public news. When they were set on intercom I guess they were voice activated, since the switch from sending to receiving was automatic. Also, if it was set on one of the other two frequencies and a message came in on the intercom frequency, there was an override to let us know to switch it to intercom.

We hardly looked at each other while we hooked them on. Sometimes the light banter comes easily, before a battle or a raid, and sometimes it doesn't. This time it didn't. Maybe because this time we had more at stake than just our own lives or the lives of strangers. Our own personal hostages to fortune were on the front lines this time. It wasn't a comfortable thought. Hell, I hadn't even known I *had* any hostages to fortune.

No sounds reached us from inside the station, not even the quiet thrum of engines that is usually audible anywhere on a space station. We had already agreed on our individual search areas, so there was nothing left to do but open the hatch to the air lock and start looking.

Michael looked like he wanted to say something, but there wasn't anything to say. He must have figured that out, because after a moment he gave himself a little shake, noticed I was watching him, smiled vaguely and not at all convincingly, and turned expectantly toward the hatch. I glanced at Jamin to make sure he was ready, then hit the release, and we all floated over to watch the hatch cover open. There wasn't really any danger yet; even if the terrorists knew we were there, they'd be waiting beyond the inner hatch cover on the other side of the air lock. But I noticed I wasn't the only one who waited with one hand on a weapon.

They didn't know we were there. The inner hatch cover opened onto a dim, deserted corridor that stretched away into the silent distance without a sign of recent habitation. Only about every third or fourth light was working, and since Newhome had been built in the early days of space colonization, before people got accustomed to living in freefall, all the lights were on one wall—they'd have called it the ceiling, when it was built—and all the handholds were on the two adjoining walls, so they cast weird elongated shadows across the fourth wall, the one the original inhabitants probably called the floor or deck.

Those early pioneers must have felt confused and discomfitted when they happened to enter, as we did, upside down with respect to the lights and handholds. Our faces, already drawn with tension, became grotesquely shadowed masks when they were lit from below by the first light inside the corridor, which happened to be one of the ones still working. None of us said anything, but we all three promptly turned over. If anyone had asked, I'd have said I did it to get the light out of my eyes. The fact was, I'd felt wrongside up, and just never mind how illogical that is in freefall.

It made me think about the courage of the pioneers. Belters always live on the edge of death; men are puny creatures, shockingly vulnerable in the harsh environment of space; but to live as we do, we don't need the kind of courage the pioneers had. We know we have Death for a neighbor, but we also know that if we keep the fences in good repair, the relationship won't get cozy. And we know how to keep the fences in repair. We know what the dangers are; the pioneers found them for us.

There was nobody even to name the hazards for them. Oh, they knew the major ones before they left Earth: they knew they had to guard against the vacuum, and against radiation belts, and wild rocks. But even the methods of protecting against those most obvious hazards were untried, uncertain, and unreliable, once. Air filters had to be designed. Air mixtures had to be tried. Alloys, engines, and equipment had to be tested. And while much of it could be tested on Earth, and in unmanned flights beyond Earth's atmosphere, there still was always a time when the first man or woman had to trust his or her life to something no man or woman had used in space before.

On top of all that, they were all born and raised on Earth, in Earth's relentless gravity well; and when they had climbed up out of it on their fiery rockets and desperate missiles, they had to figure out how to create artificial gravity by primitive means, or live in freefall. Naturally enough, they opted for gravity whenever they could. The problems caused by Coriolis force were minor compared to the strange wonder of that state they called "weightlessness" or "zero gravity." Of course the state wasn't weightless; they just hadn't learned to measure weight in the absence of their accustomed gravity well; and there is no "zero gravity"; there is only distance from objects massive enough to produce discernable gravity. The orbit of a freefall station depends on gravity. But the very imprecision of the words they used shows how alien the environment was to them; and yet, they managed to live in it. They and their descendants managed, in the face of unimaginable difficulty and uncertainty, to put colonies in space, then on the moon, on Mars, and eventually in the asteroid belt.

If I, who had spent at least half my life in freefall, felt uncomfortable when I entered one of their corridors with my feet toward what they had considered the ceiling, how must they have felt, every day of their lives?

The handholds on the walls were hard metal things, like widely spaced ladder rungs. I found myself actually clinging to each I touched, rather than just pushing along the way one usually does. It wasn't only because of my sympathy for history, though I could well imagine that a nervous pioneer, perhaps afraid of being caught in the middle of the corridor with nothing to push against but air, might have grasped each handhold gratefully as he reached it; I needed the feel of the cold rungs under my hands to steady me for a much different reason. I had the shakes.

I hadn't expected that. I think every pilot must get the shakes after a bad run or a difficult docking, when the adrenaline rush of excitement and fear wears off and reaction sets in. But we'd been luckier than I'd dared hope, docking so gently we hadn't disturbed the equilibrium of the station or even of the unit we'd docked on, and then finding that unit empty of terrorists when we got inside. We weren't safe yet, by a long shot, but we had been granted an unexpected breathing space; and perhaps because it *was* unexpected, I was reacting badly.

At that moment, I'd have actually welcomed a run-in with the terrorists. It's as well we didn't get it, though, because it would have botched what plans we had. The most important thing was to find the hostages before the terrorists found us. If we had to fight our way out of the station, we'd manage; at least we'd know where we were going. But until we were ready to leave, the search for the hostages would be greatly simplified if we didn't also have to fight off terrorists.

The first junction in that corridor was where I left Michael and Jamin. They were to search Units Two and Five, for which the junctions were farther along Unit Seven's corridor. I'd drawn Unit Four, which seemed to me the likeliest one. The master controls were in Unit One, and the flight deck in Unit Six; Unit Four was directly between them. Two and Five adjoined Four, and were good possibilities because they were near both the control room and the flight deck, but they had both originally been living quarters, with lots of separate chambers opening onto central corridors. Michael said that made them perfect for stashing hostages. I thought if I wanted to stash a large group of hostages quickly, where I could easily keep track of them all, I'd want them in a storage or clearing area where they could be lumped together for guarding. Unit Four had been the central clearing area for everything that came through the flight deck. The whole unit had only eight chambers, though the designers had carefully separated them by running three corridors right through the center of the unit, so they crossed at right angles in a big open space in the middle.

I made my entrance at the end of one of those corridors. Like Unit Seven's corridor, it was lighted only on one side, with handholds on the adjoining sides and nothing on the fourth side. I didn't have to turn over, this time; the corridors were aligned so the lighted side was the same in both units. I wondered what they'd done with the third corridor in Unit

Four. Logically, the one that crossed this one on the same plane would have its lights on the same side, but what about the one that crossed them at what might be called the vertical? If these two had an "up" side and a "down" side, the third one would have an "up" end, and a "down" end. Since I thought it unlikely that they'd have put lights on only one wall at one end of a rather long corridor, I wondered whether they'd have hit on the solution common in modern freefall corridors; lights on all sides.

Fascinating as the speculation was, I didn't devote much attention to it; if this was the unit in which the hostages were being held, it would be patrolled. Even if it weren't, I might run into random terrorists wandering between the flight deck and control room. Nor was this corridor as conveniently shadowed as the one in Unit Seven; the light fixtures were modern. The kind that don't burn out. Every one of them was working, and there were a lot of them.

There were also a lot of doors, in various sizes, and some of them were set back enough in the wall that the resultant space provided narrow hiding places. Narrow was better than none. If I heard someone coming along one of the other corridors and ducked into one of those doorways, I'd be invisible from the central area where the corridors crossed. If anyone came along my corridor, I was in trouble; but there was nothing to do about that, so I didn't worry about it.

I pressed the signal beside a door and floated cautiously to one side of the opening, out of sight from within. The Comm Link behind my ear announced, with appropriate music and stirring phrases, that Michael, Jamin, and the Skyrider were on their way to the "terrorist hideout" in a "desperate bid" to rescue the hostages. The door I'd opened let onto a vast, empty chamber, lighted at intervals and crossed with shadows. I closed it and moved to the other side of the corridor to try the door there.

The newscaster behind my ear began a somewhat distorted retelling of the *Marabou* incident. I tapped it irritably to see if the terrorists had anything more interesting to talk about, but they weren't talking. The second door I tried didn't open on command. That seemed promising, till I noticed that it had been permanently bonded shut. It didn't look like recent work. I pushed on toward the next one on that side.

I had just tried the third door I'd found when a pair of long-haired, long-legged women wearing work suits and bristling with Colonial Army weapons floated silently around a corner into my corridor. The door I had just signaled was sliding obediently open in smooth, efficient silence, and the chamber beyond would have been a perfect place to hide; but it was already occupied by hostages and their guards.

CHAPTER NINE

The approaching women hadn't seen me. I pushed
the signal again, and the door to the hostage chamber
reversed its motion, sliding quietly shut. There were
no sudden sounds from within: perhaps nobody had
noticed the movement of the door. I'd had only a
brief glimpse of the people inside, and couldn't remember for sure whether any of them had been
looking my way. Since I heard nothing from them,
the two women approaching along the corridor seemed
the more immediate hazard. I pressed my back against
the door and put my hand on my weapon.

Even if I'd been able to stay absolutely rigid, not
breathing, I couldn't have stayed hidden long in that
shallow depression in the wall. The harder I tried to
press back against the panel behind me, the more I
tended to float back out into the corridor. For every
action there is an equal and opposite reaction. I left
my weapon in its holster and used both hands to
wedge myself back against the door panel.

If the women kept coming, I would have to shoot it out with them; but there was a small chance they might turn off into one of the chambers along the way before they got near enough to see me. While I wasn't worried about whether I could take them if I had to, it would be more pleasant for all concerned if I didn't have to: particularly since the ensuing ruckus might alert the guards inside the chamber with the hostages, and then I'd really have a fight on my hands.

It didn't quite come to that. I was just getting ready to let go the sides of the doorway and grab for my handgun when the personal Comm behind my ear, which I had left set on the terrorist frequency, squawked some harried nonsense about the Colonial Fleet that made the two approaching women grab for the nearest handholds to turn themselves around and dive back down the corridor the way they had come. Since they couldn't have heard my Comm, they must have had some of their own; and whatever had been said about the Colonial Fleet, which I hadn't quite caught because I was concentrating too hard on how I was going to swing out from hiding and stun two women before they could blast me, must have been pretty important. I've seldom seen anyone overcome inertia so neatly as to get turned all the way around and going the other way that quickly in freefall. They didn't get very tangled in the turnaround, either. They were Earthers, but they hadn't spent all their time before this in gravity.

The Comm spoke again. I tapped it to the intercom frequency and propelled myself across the corridor to try a door on that side, hoping for an empty chamber in which to conceal myself while I called Jamin and Michael. The door I tried opened smoothly, revealing a nearly empty chamber. There were a few crates stuck to retaining pillars near one wall, casting dark shadows across the still air of the rest of the chamber, but no sign of people. I swung through the opening, caught a handhold inside, and hit the door signal to close it. Then it occurred to me that it would be a good idea to be able to watch the corridor, so I let go my handhold and kicked on into the chamber, looking for something loose and small with which I could prop the door open a crack. Meantime, under my breath, I said, "Jamin. Michael. They're in Unit Four, chamber six. Come and get them."

Jamin's voice, thin and crackly through the tiny speaker, said, "On my way."

There was no response from Michael. After a few more tries, I quit calling him. I'd found a prybar in a tool rack next to a pillar of crates, and I took it back over to the door. Getting the door open far enough to prop, and closed again on the prybar before anybody in the corridor might notice, was tricky. It turned out there wasn't anybody in the corridor to notice, but I didn't know that when I started.

While I waited for Jamin to arrive, I told him as much as I could from the brief glimpse I'd got of the hostage chamber. There were perhaps eight or ten adult hostages, and as many children of varying ages, which sounded like the right numbers and must mean they'd been all lumped together; I'd been afraid some might have been separated out and require an additional search.

"How many guards with them?" asked Jamin.

"Four that I saw. There could be more. I only had a quick look at the chamber before I was interrupted."

"Interrupted how?"

"Never mind. Wait a minute; something's happening.'' Through the propped-open crack in the door beside me, I saw three guards coming out of the hostage chamber. They disappeared from my sight, apparently headed for the flight deck; and after a moment, three more came out. They paused by the door to hold a quick conference. Their gestures were animated, but they spoke in angry undertones so I couldn't make out the words. One of them thought about hitting another; he braced himself on two hand-holds for the purpose, but was discouraged by the third, and there was a lot of head shaking and weapon waving for a few more seconds before finally one of them shrugged in resignation and waved the other two away.

They went the way the first three had gone, toward the flight deck. The one who remained hung uneasily next to the door, his attention more on the corridor where the others had gone than on the door behind him, where the hostages were stashed. I told Jamin, briefly, what had happened. ''I think the one who stayed is all the guard they've left on the hostages. They're making this easy: if I stun him, I can get the hostages out, and we'll all meet you in Unit Seven.''

''I'm not in Unit Seven. Wait till I get there.''

''If I do, he'll see you the minute you enter this corridor, and I know I said he'd distracted, but he's not that distracted. Besides, he won't expect anybody coming out of the chamber I'm in. I can probably stun him without even exposing myself.'' I hoped I could, because I'd had time by now to see that he wasn't carrying a stun gun; he had a laser.

''Skyrider,'' said Jamin.

''Hang loose.'' I braced myself. The door, when I had opened it to get into this chamber, had moved in perfect silence. I put my hand on the prybar I had used to prop it open, so I could keep it from banging against anything when I opened the door again and the prop floated loose. Then I changed my mind and decided to hang onto my weapon; I needed one hand for the door signal, and a weapon seemed the logical choice for the other. If I used it quickly and efficiently enough, I wouldn't care how much noise the prybar might make.

The guard inadvertently made it even easier for me. He must have got worried about the hostages; because he turned around, opened the hostage chamber, looked inside, and closed the door again. While he was still involved in getting turned back around to watch the corridor, I hit my door signal and propelled myself out into the corridor. He never had a chance. He barely got his laser clear of its holster before I stunned him.

I left him floating limply along the corridor while I opened the hostage chamber. Inside, the first impression I got was of a tangled mass of people, children and adults alike, all huddled together in the center of a large, otherwise empty chamber. The lights were working in here, too, and they cast a pitiless pale wash over all the faces, so that at first all I could see were staring eyes and open mouths in pale ovals that jutted out here and there from the tangle of arms and legs; and every one of them was looking at me. It was positively spooky. The darker faces made it eerier still by being less visible against the glitter and dark of party clothing, so that they kept popping into visual resolution, all staring eyes in sinister ovals of shadow, after I'd got used to the paler faces.

It hadn't occurred to me, when I went tearing in there with my stun gun drawn, that the majority of these people had never seen me before and had no idea who I was or why I was there. Moreover, I was wearing the standard Belter costume I'd put on for the party, and that was how several of the terrorists I'd seen had been dressed. For all these people knew, I had come to stun the lot of them, and maybe space them. They'd seen their guards go out in a state of agitation. They might guess someone had arrived to save them, and that the terrorists would get rid of them before anyone else could reach them.

At least I'd been right in guessing there would be no more guards inside. I said quickly, "It's all right, people," because I saw one or two people on the far side of the tangle carefully extricating themselves, and in the face of what they probably saw as certain death, they just might have the courage to try to overpower me. "I'm not a terrorist. I'm the—"

I didn't get a chance to finish: Collis saw me. "Skyrider!" he shouted, and came hurtling out of the crowd like a missile, straight into my arms. It was all I could do to hang onto my weapon, and both of us bounced off the wall before we stopped tumbling. "See," he said triumphantly, his blue eyes flashing in the light. "I *told* you my dad and the Skyrider would save us." He looked at me, suddenly uncertain. "Where is my dad?"

"He'll be along." In the massed crowd of hostages, there were some still tumbling from the force of Collis's exit. "Did you kick off people?" I asked him.

He looked startled, then guilty. "I guess I did. There wasn't anything else."

"Never mind." I let him go and got myself turned to face the hostages. "Okay, folks, first things first: let's get you out of here before your guards get back from lunch."

"They didn't go to lunch," said Collis.

"No? Do you know where they did go?"

"Sure. The Colonial Fleet is coming, and they've gone in case they have to fight them off if they attack. They argued about it, because they all wanted to go, and one of them had to stay here, outside the door, did you stun that one? And they couldn't decide which one."

I sorted out the pronouns as best I could. "Okay. Then they may not be back so soon. Come on, folks, let's see if you can get yourselves untangled and ready to go. I did stun the guard outside, but there's no guarantee there aren't more coming."

While they were sorting themselves out, I switched my Comm back to public news to see if I could find out what was going on outside. I could. The Earthers had spotted the Colonial Fleet we'd heard assembling on our way out here, and—surprise!—Earth just happened to have a fleet of her own all ready and waiting for a signal to come chase Colonials. Apparently the signal had been given. The newscaster said the Colonial Fleet was already here, and the Earth Fighters would be here soon.

Station Newhome was getting caught between two trigger-happy fleets just delighted at the chance to be in on the first battle of the long-expected war. At the smallest provocation, they would start blasting each other out of space, and I doubted whether the terrorists could or would keep them from blasting Station Newhome while they were about it.

I switched back to intercom to call Michael and Jamin again. Michael still didn't answer. Jamin was about to enter Unit Four. "Go carefully," I said. "Have you been listening to the news?"

"I heard it," he said.

"The terrorists heard it, too. God knows what they'll be doing. Try not to run into any. Which reminds me, have you seen any sign of Michael?"

"None."

"I'm sorting out the hostages now. We should be ready to leave in a few minutes. How soon can you get here?"

"One minute."

He was as good as his word. The hostages weren't all organized to leave the chamber before he got there. Collis greeted him with, if anything, even more enthusiasm than that with which he had greeted me. Jamin almost got knocked right back into the corridor when he entered the chamber. I grinned at him and introduced him to the erstwhile hostages: "This is your rescue pilot. Do what he tells you, and you may get off this station alive."

"You're coming with us, aren't you?" asked Collis.

"No." I looked at Jamin. "Give me ten minutes, after you reach the *Defiance*. If I'm not back by then, disengage without me."

For just a moment he looked at me with the cold, impersonal arrogance with which he habitually concealed personal discomfort, and I thought he was going to argue. But there wasn't time for that. He drew a breath, gave me a weary little grin, and nodded. "Okay."

"I think we'd better dispense with the Comms from now on, too, or anyway use the intercom frequency as little as possible. As soon as the terrorists find out they've lost their hostages, they'll be listening for intruders. I hope to hell they don't know about that shuttle dock."

He gave me an odd look. "Even if they do, I doubt if they'll guess we used it."

"Oh, hell, dead-docking isn't all that big a deal,"
I said. "Besides, the public news announced we
were coming, and everybody knows I can dead-dock
fairly well."

"All the more reason to be careful." He looked
troubled. "Damn it. I'll go with you."

"Then who'll fly the hostages home?"

"There must be a pilot—"

"No way. Nobody flies the *Defiance* but us." I
grinned at him. "Besides, I checked their records.
There's no shuttle pilot here. Right, guys?" I looked
at the hostages. Nobody contradicted me. "You see,"
I said. "Now go, before new guards show up."

They went. Collis carried Michael's young son
again. One of the erstwhile hostages collected the
laser that the guard at the door had dropped when I
stunned him. She brought up the rear of the party,
brandishing her weapon as though it were a talisman
against evil. All their bright finery looked frayed and
tarnished now, as worn by the hours of terror as their
tense faces and haunted eyes. If the terrorists caught
sight of them, they hadn't a chance. Most of them
knew it. They were resigned to death, by now. But
they floated bravely down that corridor without a
whimper. The illusion of positive action. They were
doing something at last. Maybe it would help.

I turned away from them toward Unit Two, where
Michael ought to be. The chance of finding him and
getting him safely off the station was even less than
Jamin's party had of reaching the *Defiance* unob-
served. But there was a chance. And I'm as suscepti-
ble as anyone to the illusion of positive action. I
would do something. Maybe it would help.

CHAPTER TEN

Unit Two was well lighted in the modern way, with lights on all sides of the corridors and pliable plastic handholds instead of the hard metal ladderlike rungs in the other units I'd seen. It was also crawling with terrorists. I hovered at the end of a corridor for several minutes, watching them, wondering what to do next, before it finally occurred to me that if there were so many of them, they couldn't possibly all know each other personally. Which should mean that they wouldn't know, on sight, that I wasn't one of them.

The unit seemed to be their living quarters. People were going in and out of the chambers and along the corridors, some chatting, some in busy silence, all carrying weapons, but none looking particularly alert or nervous. Obviously they didn't expect any intruders here. That was a distinct advantage for me: people often don't see what they don't expect to see. I was armed, I was dressed like some of them, and if I

acted as though I belonged there, they would probably assume I did.

Anyway, it was a chance, and I had to take it. The
major problem with it was, if Michael were here and
they hadn't caught him, why didn't he respond when
I called him? And if they *had* caught him, why
weren't they looking for further intruders? Even if he
told them he worked alone, they wouldn't believe it.
Besides everything else, there was that damn newscaster. He'd told them we were coming. If they
found one of us, they'd know the other two of us
were aboard, somewhere.

If I waited much longer, I'd get the shakes again. I
felt unexpectedly nervous and uncertain, like a green
recruit on her first mission. Part of it was not knowing what was going on outside, but knowing that it
might very well be war. I had been too long im-
mersed in matters of war. It wasn't that I was worried they'd start it without me, so much as it was that
I felt somehow personally connected with the proposed battle. As though they *couldn't* start it without
me. Or as though, should they start it without me,
something would go terribly wrong with the universe. Of course that was nonsense. But I wasn't
thinking of sense or the lack of it. I was thinking of
all the years of waiting, wondering, warding off war
and knowing my life was ultimately directed toward
nothing but war. I had avoided the last one, and then
become a fierce and efficient warrior, in a time of
uneasy peace. Now that the new war might be at
hand I felt confused and startled not to be at the
center of things.

Well, if I thought I was such a great fighting
machine, surely I could take on a few terrorists, to
rescue Michael. If I really was as good as I thought I

was, it shouldn't even come to a fight. Not all battles are fought with lasers and stun guns, and not all battlefields look like what they are. Nor all warriors, come to that.

I holstered my gun and glided nonchalantly into the corridor of Unit Two, past a group of Martian-garbed terrorists who didn't even look my way. I was all set to nod and smile at them, or to quick-draw and stun them, and they didn't even notice me. The corridor was shiny plasteel between the lights. My reflection lumbered along with me, hazy and inter-rupted. Most of the doors along the way were open, showing cramped living quarters, each chamber hung with two hammocks and sporting little nests of per-sonal belongings that hadn't been properly stowed in the wall compartments, but only stuck haphazardly to retaining panels.

If Michael were in such a chamber, it would of course be closed and locked: closed, anyway, if he were hiding and not caught. I didn't bother with more than a cursory glance at the open chambers, since he wouldn't be there. And I couldn't open the closed ones, in case there were people inside. One time, or even twice, I could pretend I'd got the wrong door and maybe even get away with it; but if anybody in the corridor noticed me going along re-peatedly opening the wrong doors, I'd be caught as surely as Michael must have been. And if he had been caught, I didn't think they'd have kept him in Unit Two. They would have taken him to their com-mand post, probably, to see what their officers could learn from him.

The command post would be in Unit One with the controls. I reached that decision and the corridor junction both at once, and swung purposefully around the corner, exactly into the arms of the first really alert group I'd seen among them.

There wasn't time to think about it. Maybe I could have brazened my way past them with some excuse, but I often move faster than I think. I had my gun out before I knew I was reaching for it. And at exactly that moment, to complicate matters, an alarm went off all around us. It was an earshaking klaxon interspersed with comments by a tinny computer voice: "Intruder alert. Blaat!! Hostages missing. Blaat!! Intruder alert. Blaat!!"

There were three terrorists facing me, armed with lasers and riot guns against my puny little stun gun. They'd known the moment I ran into them that I wasn't a terrorist, and the intruder alert confirmed it. But though they were quick enough to identify me, they were peacetime soldiers; and they hadn't had the time I'd had to adjust to the loss of peace. They weren't accustomed to the idea of shooting people. What if, by some wild chance, it were a mistake? They would look foolish; they would be reprimanded; they'd have killed someone who shouldn't have died.

That hesitation was all the help I needed. Not one of them got a weapon drawn before I'd stunned them all. Behind me, in the corridor I'd just left, I could hear people reacting to the intruder alert. Some of them would realize they'd seen me pass. I had seconds, at best, to get out of sight; and while any handy chamber would have hidden me for a little while, I'd have been trapped in it. I couldn't hold them off forever. I grabbed up one of the riot guns and holstered my stun gun; the time for gentle peacetime weapons was over.

Unit Two was a maze of corridors and interconnected chambers. If I could get off the main corridors, into some of the small maintenance creepways between chambers, I'd have a good chance of working my way into Unit One without getting caught. But first I had to find the maintenance creepways, and then I had to remember where they led.

Somebody shouted behind me, and I grabbed instinctively for one of the terrorists I'd stunned. There wasn't much sense in it, since I didn't think they would prove to be sentimental folks on the whole, once they got over that initial uncertainty over whether the battle had properly started; but I thrust her bodily between me and the group behind me anyway. I was trying frantically to recall the blueprints I'd examined, to remember which chamber might let onto the maintenance tunnels. The one next to me? Or the one two doors down?

I'd been right about their general sentimentality. They hadn't any. The one I'd put up as a shield hardly slowed her fellows at all. They burned her without hesitation in their effort to get at me. However, even if she failed as an emotional barrier, she was a good temporary physical one. Under cover of her charred, recoiling body, I kicked my way down the corridor and around another corner. At that, one of my arms got singed, but not badly enough to make me drop the riot gun I'd stolen. I paused at the corner to aim it back at the terrorists, and was pleased to hear the blast connect.

There was a hatch to the maintenance tunnels right in the new corridor I'd chosen. Quickly, before they could get to the corner and see which way I'd gone, I hit the sequence to open the cover, praying the whole time that I remembered it correctly.

I did, and I swarmed feet-first in through the open-

ing before anybody entered the main corridor from
either direction to see me. Pulling the cover shut was
tricky, with one sore arm and a massive riot gun in
the way, but fear can be quite an inducement to
action. I got it shut, and relaxed in the protective
darkness, riot gun aimed at the closed hatch, wondering whether the terrorists were as familiar with the
intricacies of Station Newhome as Michael's memory
and Starkey's blueprints had made me.

Apparently they weren't. None of them tried the
hatch. Lying in that still darkness, I could hear the
familiar thrum of engines that had been missing in
Unit Seven, and that I had been too busy to notice in
the other units I'd passed through. I put out a hand to
feel the plasteel vibrate, and the motion made me
bump against the wall at my back.

The creepway was barely large enough to justify
its name: creeping was the only form of locomotion
I'd be able to manage, and I'm small. I wondered
how the regular maintenance people managed, or
whether only small people were given the job. Somewhere I'd read that our ancestors, in the time when
Station Newhome was built, were smaller than modern humans, but if they were small enough to travel
comfortably in this cramped tube, the size differential
was greater than I'd imagined.

I couldn't hear a thing from the corridor outside.
When I felt reasonably steady again, I began to
propel myself awkwardly backward, away from the
hatch, using one hand and the barrel of the riot gun
to push me along. If I kept my legs absolutely straight,
and my head ducked down between my shoulders, it
didn't matter much that I was unable to push myself
in perfectly straight glides; the tube was smooth for
the most part, with maintenance panels inset with

beveled edges, so there wasn't anything to snag on or bump against except the walls.

The darkness bothered me more than anything. The air felt close and stale, and I could feel the mass of the whole station pressing in toward that black tunnel, straining the walls around me; but I wouldn't have minded that, if I'd had even a small light to keep me company.

I'd never imagined I was afraid of the dark. Indeed, I love the dark of space. But that can hardly be called darkness, pinpointed and whitewashed as it is with the light of stars. Here I could see only blackness, and the occasional startling suggestion of light when I brushed against the walls and released stored static electricity there. My eyes pulled wide with the effort to see, till they began to ache with strain and I had to force myself to close them. I found myself pushing up against the tunnel at my back, just for the feel of reality against my tension-sensitive muscles.

An unexpected rattling clang somewhere down the tunnel behind me brought me up gasping, with my fingers clutching at the smooth edge of an inspection panel to hold me in place. *Someone was in the tunnel with me!* Involuntarily I tried to turn around, to face the danger, and banged my head hard against a wall.

I had lost the riot gun. I didn't remember dropping it, but it wasn't in my hands. I must have let go of it when the noise startled me. In trying to turn around, and recoiling from the blow to my head, I could have knocked it in any direction. My eyes went wide again, searching the impenetrable black, and I tried again to look behind me, this time by looking over my shoulder rather than turning around. The tunnel was too narrow to permit even that; and if it hadn't been, there'd have been nothing to see. I gave it up and swept my arms cautiously before me, searching for the riot gun. Nothing. Only darkness.

If I moved very slowly and carefully, I could probably draw my stun gun; but whatever danger there might be was coming from behind me, where I could neither see nor fire. And if I ever got out of this smothering closed darkness, I'd want that riot gun. Biting my lip in an effort to control my growing panic, I reached out again . . . and bumped the gun.

It had been just at the limit of my reach, and my fingers had touched it; knocked it, bouncing, against the wall and on down the tunnel the way I had come. I realized I hadn't the smallest notion exactly how far I *had* come. How long had I been creeping along in the darkness? A minute? An hour? An eternity? How far had I come, and where was I now in relation to any goal?

In that blind silence, I think I had forgotten all goals. I was trapped, embraced, enveloped by darkness, by the awful mass of a space station, by silence, by fear. I'd rather have faced a whole squadron of terrorists than spend five more minutes in that musty hole, but I no longer even knew how to get out of there.

I was fairly sure I hadn't turned any corners. Surely I'd have remembered turning a corner. Logically, then, all I had to do to get out was to go forward again, till I came to the hatch through which I had entered. Somewhere along the way, I should find the riot gun; and when I got to the hatch, and got it open, I would probably find a deserted corridor outside, from which the terrorists had all gone down other corridors in search of me.

Reassured by even such faulty reasoning, I clawed at the walls and managed, by straining my wrists and fingers, to push myself slowly back the way I had come. Travel in this direction was harder. There wasn't room to bend my knees very well, to kick with my feet, and when I tried to bend my arms, I almost broke both elbows and jammed myself permanently between them.

Once I'd worked my arms free again, I kept them and my legs straight, using only my hands and toes to push me along. It was slow going at first, but once I got properly started, inertia took over. Then it was almost as easy as going the other way had been. At least now I was going frontward. In that tight black space it didn't really matter, since I wouldn't see a hazard till I hit it, but I felt obscurely reassured to think that I would be facing it, whatever it was.

Searching for the riot gun slowed me a little. I bumped it twice more without catching it, and began to worry that when I finally came to the hatch where I had entered the tunnel, the riot gun would have got there before me, propelled by my clumsiness to knock against the hatch cover and alert the terrorists to my location.

I didn't hear it bump anything, except once, against a wall, sounding distant and echoey. After that, there was only the thrum of the engines. I didn't find the riot gun again. I didn't find the hatch through which I had entered, either. At first I kept telling myself I just hadn't gone far enough yet. I didn't know how far "far enough" would be, but I did know I had lost all track of time while I was scooting backward into blackness. Now, gliding frontward, weary of the effort and of darkness and of reaching for the riot gun I never quite caught, time stretched out interminably. Any minute now I would come to the hatch cover.

Another few meters. Another push. Another blind reach, and I would touch it.

It wasn't until I had lost all contact with the riot gun, and estimated I'd been traveling at least twice as long in this direction as I had in the other, without ever finding a hatch or a corner or any small sign of any way out of the tunnel, that I finally admitted I was lost.

CHAPTER ELEVEN

I don't panic readily. At least, that's what I tell myself; and since I'm very gullible, I believe a lot of the things I tell myself. Even then, lost in the black, cramped maintenance tubes of an antique space station, unable to locate a hatch, poorly armed and fairly sure of a hostile reaction should I find a way out, I believed it when I told myself I don't panic readily.

I also panicked. Hell, nobody's perfect. Besides, anybody might panic in a situation like that. I couldn't see: not even my hand in front of my face, had I been able to put my hand in front of my face, which I couldn't because the space was too small to bend my arm that way. I couldn't hear anything except the almost subliminal rumble of engines. I couldn't smell anything but stale air, nor taste anything but dust; and I couldn't feel anything but the smooth plasteel walls of my narrow prison. Even if I'd known exactly where I was, I'd have felt anxious about it.

Besides, logic said I *should* know where I was. I'd gone backward for a certain distance in a straight line, and then I'd gone forward for the same distance in a straight line . . . and I hadn't ended up in the same place. It didn't make any sense.

I don't believe I made the situation any worse by panicking. I already didn't know where I was. After I'd scrambled frantically along for a while, barking my knuckles on the walls and wrenching a knee in an effort to travel faster, I still didn't know where I was. I gained nothing by it, but I lost nothing, either, except a little time and self-respect. In that place, time didn't mean much, anyway; and self-respect may not have been the least of my worries, but it certainly didn't head the list.

Actually, it was wrenching my knee that led to my discovery of what had happened. It hurt, and I tried to twist around to reach for it. By all rights I should have banged my head against the wall again, but I didn't. I folded right into a sitting position without bumping anything, till the inertia of my headlong travel prior to the sitting trick brought my back up hard against what appeared to be a wall in the middle of the tunnel.

Startled, I forgot all about my knee. Even if I had somehow got turned around enough to come up against a side wall, I shouldn't have had room to do it in a seated position. I thought for a moment I must have found a corner where the tunnel turned at a sharp right angle, and I'd come on it just right to bend at the waist without banging my head; but when I reached overhead, I hit a wall. At a right angle turn, I shouldn't have had room to fold up like that, anyway, without doing it carefully right along the wall of the tunnel; the thing was only inches wider than I was; and,

having done it, I should have felt nothing overhead
but tunnel. There shouldn't be room to bring my
knee up against my chest, but there was. I'd thought
a corner would be even more claustrophobic than the
straight tunnel itself; that was why I'd been sure I
couldn't have passed one without noticing it.

Puzzled, I reached behind me to feel the thing I'd
come up against. It was smoothly rounded, and it
ended just below my shoulders. Below that, there
was emptiness: more tunnel. Edging feet-first back
into the tunnel I'd come through, I stretched my body
out again and kept both hands on the side walls while
I crept forward, and met with no resistance. When I
reached above me again, I hit the wall. Thoroughly
confused now, I pressed my hands harder against the
wall to stop my forward motion, and then crept
slowly backward, this time running one hand along
the wall above me. It tapered away from me in a neat
rounded curve, till I couldn't reach it any longer. For
a space of two or three meters there was emptiness;
then I felt the wall again, tapering back down toward
me.

It was a Y intersection of two tunnels, curved so
gently that I'd have passed it without noticing if I
hadn't tried to bend at exactly the right moment. Now
that I knew what it was, I finally remembered the
strange curving lines of the mainenance tubes on the
blueprint I'd studied. I hadn't expected to do any
traveling in them, so I hadn't committed their eccentricities perfectly to memory. Another lesson in pre-
paring for the unexpected. Now I knew how I'd got
lost: I could have passed any number of those intersections, going either direction, without knowing it.
But I still didn't know the way out.

I did feel better, though. The nightmare bewilderment was gone. I had a logical explanation for what had happened. Logic is a wonderful thing. Very bracing. I didn't have any more idea how to find my way out of those tubes than I'd had a few minutes ago. I was still trapped in the claustrophobic darkness with no idea where I was or where I was going. But the fear was gone. I was back in a world that made sense.

For a few minutes I just floated there at the junction of the two tunnels and enjoyed the knowledge that logic still worked. Then I began to use it. I could maneuver pretty well in the open space of the junction: enough to turn clear around without straining myself, if I was careful. I was careful. Besides not wanting to break or bruise anything, I didn't want to lose the junction by inadvertently propelling myself down one of the tunnels before I'd decided which I wanted to take.

Putting my head up each of the tunnels in turn told me very little. They all smelled the same. I couldn't see any difference in the quality of the darkness, nor feel any markings that might indicate where any of them led. There were no air currents to follow. I thought one of them had more engine noise in it than the other two, but the difference was so small I couldn't be sure of it. I knew, of course, that the hatch by which I had entered was back the way I had come, and around some corner I hadn't noticed, but I also knew there would be other hatches along the other tunnels that I would have just as much chance of finding.

The riot gun was well and truly lost. It might be somewhere along the tunnel through which I'd come, but it was almost certainly around a corner on a side tunnel, and there could be a lot of those. To set out in that direction only because I wanted the gun would have been idiotic.

However, I also wanted Unit One; and as nearly as I could guess, one tunnel led more in its direction than the other two. Moreover, that tunnel was the one with possibly greater engine noise. Unit One housed some of the main engines for the whole station. Even if I had entirely lost my sense of direction in my panicky rush through the tunnels, which I might well have done, the engine noise was a reasonable clue to follow.

I went head first, and I avoided the long frictionless glides that had got me here; they were also what had got me past at least one and probably several unnoticed intersections. In order to keep contact with the walls on all sides, I injected a deliberate spin into my forward motion, and trailed my hands along the walls as I went. The effort to maintain the spin made travel more difficult, and the friction of dragging the backs of my fingers lightly along the walls made it slower still; but it worked. I hadn't gone far at all when I detected the next intersection, and this time two of the tunnels were going in the general direction I wanted.

Keeping my toes in contact with the curved wall at the intersection, I slid the length of my body up one of the tunnels, then pulled myself back and tried the other. The second one seemed just faintly louder. I took it. And had to make the choice again, three times more, before I found a recognizable hatch cover to let me out of the darkness. I never did find the riot gun.

By the time I'd located the hatch release mechanism, I was so eager to get out of there that it was all I could do to relax and listen for a while before I punched the release code. I couldn't hear anything beyond the hatch, but that didn't mean anything; there might have been a roaring party of rioting Belters on the other side and I wouldn't have heard them through the cover. If somebody had been actively engaged in opening the hatch, I might have heard that. I didn't, so I released the hatch cover and waited again; it had made an audible response, clicking as little hidden tabs slid out of their locking slots, and I wanted to see whether anyone besides me had heard it.

Apparently nobody did, since nobody jerked the cover off and fired a laser in my face, so I went ahead and cracked the hatch just enough to let in a narrow band of light. Even that was enough to blind me. I blinked and squinted and waited. Still no sound outside.

From my vantage point, I couldn't tell whether the hatch opened onto a corridor or a chamber. There was a chance that it would open into a chamber that was locked from the outside, which would mean I would have to get back into the maintenance tubes and try again, since without the riot gun I couldn't break a chamber lock to get outside. I chose not to think about that. If it happened, I would deal with it, but I wouldn't like it. I preferred to imagine that the hatch I'd found would open onto a nice, deserted corridor, preferably in familiar territory, so I could set right out from there to find Michael without further delay.

My ten minutes to get back to the *Defiance* must have run out long since. It occurred to me, while I was waiting for my eyes to adjust to light again, to wonder what was happening outside. I'd had my Comm on the terrorist frequency; but either they'd been very quiet, or the walls of the maintenance tube had insulated me from their signal. Now I switched to the public news frequency and discovered that, as expected, the two opposing fleets had arrived at Station Newhome and were even now facing off against each other, with Newhome and the terrorists—and me—between them.

Either Jamin hadn't disengaged with the erstwhile hostages, or he had neglected to mention it to either fleet; there was nothing about rescued hostages on the news, though there was rampant speculation about the rescue attempt. Jamin would probably stretch the ten minutes, to give me a better chance. If that was what he was doing, I hoped he didn't try to stretch them too far. The terrorists might not believe anybody could dead-dock at the shuttle dock on Unit Seven, but I was willing to bet they'd go look to make sure. For everybody's continued happiness, it would be best if the *Defiance* weren't there when they looked.

I worked my stun gun out of its holster and aimed it at the center of the hatch before I pushed the cover all the way back. It was a wasted gesture. The corridor before me was as empty as I'd hoped. Even better, it was familiar; not from recent experience, but from the maps and blueprints in the *Defiance*'s computer. There were six walls instead of four. Only Unit Three had hexagonal corridors. And Unit Three was directly connected to Unit One. Moreover, it seemed as abandoned and forgotten as Unit Seven. I could hardly have selected a better place to exit the tubes if I'd had my choice of the whole station.

Still holding the stun gun ready, I propelled myself forward, out of the tube, and caught the hatch cover to hold me steady while I surveyed the corridor.

Fully half the lights were out, and there was nobody in sight. Bracing myself on a metal handhold, I pushed the hatch shut and locked it.

So far, in my search for Michael, I had behaved quite stupidly. I decided maybe from now on I should stop that.

Sure. And if they shoot you, don't die. Well, hell. Resolutions are good for the soul . . . as long as one doesn't take them too seriously.

The newscaster behind my ear began yet another rendition of the *Marabou* incident, and I was a bit sick of hearing about the daring exploits of the remarkable Skyrider. I switched back to the terrorist frequency. They were chattering about the hostile fleets outside, but reaching no conclusions. Not unreasonable; what could they conclude? The chatter bored and distracted me, so I switched to the intercom frequency and listened to the silence.

While I was checking out the Comm Link, I was also wandering cautiously along the corridor, looking for landmarks. Unit One still seemed like the best bet in which to find Michael, and I knew Unit Three was connected with Unit One, but I had to discover where I was in Unit Three, and how to get from where I was to the entrance to Unit One.

I also had to dodge terrorists. The fact that there were none visible in Unit Three now was no guarantee that they mightn't drop in for a visit any time. I'd had quite enough of getting cornered and shot at, so I listened carefully as I went along; and kept track, this time, of all the maintenance hatches I passed; and checked every chamber door, to see which were open and what was beyond them. Most were unlocked if not actually open, and a lot of them had odds and ends of equipment and supplies stored inside that would make them difficult to search and easy to hide in. That was nice to know.

I didn't get any use out of the information, though, until I was right at the junction to Unit One. I'd known One would be thick with terrorists. I'd even guessed that the entrances from other units might be guarded. I hadn't guessed how heavily they would be guarded. Someone must have been listening to the same newscaster I had been, and believed his over-excited estimation of the wonderfulness of me. To hear him tell it, I was a strong candidate for God. (I hadn't even been aware She'd put the job up for a vote.) That might explain why the entrance to Unit One had six (count 'em six) armed guards watching over it.

They weren't trusting to small arms and riot guns, either. Three of the guards had those, and were floating patrol. The other three had side arms, and one of them had a riot gun, but they weren't floating patrol. They weren't going anywhere. They were solidly braced in position, nursemaiding a laser cannon that looked powerful enough to knock Unit Three right off the station if the guards took a sudden dislike to it for any reason. Which they probably would, if they saw me in it.

CHAPTER TWELVE

They weren't as alert as they thought they were. The heavy armament gave them a false sense of security. Even the fabled Skyrider couldn't possibly survive the blast of their laser cannon. What they forgot was that it couldn't do me a bit of harm if they didn't fire it.

I took refuge in one of the nearby chambers while I considered the possibilities. The three with the cannon were no problem; they were stationary targets. Besides, they had such touching faith in the terrible power of their weapon that they almost certainly didn't think they'd have to use it. If the Skyrider entered their corridor, by God, she'd think twice about trying to get past them.

The three who were less spectacularly armed were confident of their safe position behind the big gun. They were careless. Back there behind that cannon, what did they have to worry about? They were trading recipes or something, and a lot more interested in their conversation than they were in the corridor they were supposed to be guarding.

Unfortunately, they weren't quite careless enough to discount entirely. If all three of them had bunched up close enough to the three with the laser cannon that I could stun them all with one spray, I'd have been past them by now. But they stayed in two groups just far enough apart to require two shots. I could wipe out the group at the cannon, but I might not get the other three before they got me. And I didn't feel like getting got.

If I'd had time, I would have just settled down comfortably to wait. Sooner or later they would have all got together to discuss lunch arrangements or trade insults or get ready to meet their relief. But the longer Michael and I stayed on this station, the longer Jamin would keep a low profile, and the greater chance that the two fleets outside would start taking potshots at each other and the station. Of course, if Jamin announced the safe recovery of the hostages, the same thing might happen, which was part of why he was keeping it quiet as long as he could. Either way, time was against me. I never was much good at waiting, anyway.

The chamber in which I was concealed contained the same assortment of stored goods as I'd seen in the chambers I'd passed: loose tools floating among crates, some of which were empty and some of which weren't. The tools were useless to me; I didn't even know what most of them were for. The crates weren't much better. I thought of bombarding the waiting guards with an assortment of empty crates and trying to sneak past during the excitement, but they just might get overexcited, and start using that damn cannon. For all I knew, it really might knock Unit

Three right off the station, and me with it. The guards would die, too, in that event, but if they got flustered enough to use the cannon, they wouldn't think of that.

Since the empty crates seemed useless, I examined the full ones. Maybe this was the chamber in which the Colonists who had defended the station during the war had stored their excess weapons, and I'd find a nice laser cannon of my own, or at least a riot gun.

I didn't find either of those, but I did find a whole crate of loaded sealant bottles in good condition and ready to use. Sealant is a foul gray substance that comes out of the nozzle as a viscous foam that adheres to nearly anything it touches. Within a fraction of a second it hardens where it hits, forming a permanent bond. It's used to seal holed bulkheads, and I've patched sizable holes with the stuff. It works. The one thing it doesn't stick to with any real conviction is people, but that was okay. I didn't want to smother the guards to death in neat little personalized coffins. I just wanted to prevent them from killing me.

First I got one of the empty crates and wedged it against a retaining pillar. Then I got a bottle of sealant, inverted it, and directed the resultant foam onto the outside of the crate; each bottle contained a miniature, manually activated grav plate, so it would work as well in freefall as in gravity. When I was finished, I had an ugly gray lump of a crate, open on one side and thoroughly coated with sealant on the others. It would make a passable shield, being impervious to just about anything short of a blast from that laser cannon itself.

Inside the crate, I stacked up a row of sealant bottles, ready for use. They'll spray a fair distance once they're inverted, and the stuff that comes out is damned obnoxious till it hardens. The fumes are acrid and foul, and the stuff itself feels disgustingly warm and slimy against human skin.

It would stick to the terrorists' clothing, of course; and if they panicked, they might get themselves stuck to a wall or a weapon. But I wasn't counting on that. I'd be happy if they just got disorganized enough to let me stun them so I could pass.

When I had my improvised war wagon ready, I took hold of it by both sides and kicked toward the chamber door. Nobody noticed when the door opened. I gathered myself for a long distance dive: I had to get near that laser cannon to put it out of action, before anybody got the suicidal urge to use it. With one hand on the box and one on a bottle of sealant, I kicked off the doorway straight down the corridor toward the cannon.

The floating patrol didn't notice me at first. There were two men and a woman at the laser cannon. One of the men saw me straight away, but he didn't know what he was seeing, and couldn't figure out how to react. I could just see him past my improvised armor. From his point of view, my crate must have looked like a blob of hardened sealant gone on a rampage. I doubt if he noticed there was anyone behind it. I kept my body stretched out flat behind it, so there wasn't much of me to see.

By the time he thought to mention my approach to the others, they'd seen me. The woman made an abortive movement toward the cannon, paused, and then just stared at me in perplexity. The second man didn't even move. He just stared.

Beyond them, the floating patrol had finally noticed me, and they were a little quicker to action.

One of them shouted something. The other two fired on me. But I had succeeded in getting right up to the cannon, and I didn't have time to worry about smaller arms just then.

I inverted a bottle of sealant and jammed its nozzle down the barrel of the cannon hard enough that it caught. The pressure of escaping sealant might force it loose again, but I hoped enough sealant would get in to render the cannon useless. Anyway, it was useless against me; I was too close to it now.

My crate still protected me from the floating patrol, and the guards whose duty was to use the cannon had only just now remembered that they had smaller arms as well. By the time they got them out and ready to use, I'd splattered them all thoroughly with foam from the second bottle of sealant.

The man who had noticed me first, as I was coming along the corridor toward them, was also the first to leave: he found sealant so repellent that he dropped his weapon and retreated down the corridor, shouting and trying frantically to wipe off the gray foam where it touched his skin. It came off readily enough, filling the air around him with lumpy globules in various stages of hardening. He looked like a man fleeing from his own personal, miniature flurry of wild rocks.

The woman at the cannon was made of sterner stuff: she ignored the foam and tried to kill me. Her laser blasts singed the hardened foam on the front of my crate, but I put a stop to that by covering her laser with foam. Without waiting to see how she'd take it, I turned to the third cannon-tender. He had a riot gun. I barely got my crate between it and me in time. The force of the blast knocked the crate away from me, but in the second it took him to correct his aim, I coated him and his weapon with the last sealant from that bottle.

There were still two bottles on the crate, and I'd meant to use them, but now I'd lost the crate. The three floating guards were too far apart to stun with one spray. One of them, a man in a Belter's costume, had taken refuge in a chamber doorway and was taking potshots at me with his laser. It was sheer luck that he was a lousy shot. There wasn't anything I could do about him for the moment but hope he didn't get any better. It wasn't likely that he would: a hand-held laser is not an easy weapon to master.

The other two guards were both women, both in Martian costumes, and both much better shots than their male companion. One of them singed my tunic. The other burned a healthy chunk off my left thigh. I stunned her first; she seemed the worst hazard. The one in the doorway kept shooting. He'd burned a hole in one of the cannon-tenders, and left a lot of burn scars on the walls, but he didn't get me. I ignored him.

The remaining cannon-tender, the one who had neither fled nor got shot by his fellow terrorists, was disentangling himself from his sealant-coated riot gun. The floating guard in the Martian costume took another shot at me just as I dived toward him. She singed my flight boot. I grabbed the cannon-tender and lifted him bodily between me and her. She shot him, too. He still made a passable shield. I kept his lifeless body between us while I kicked off the cannon toward her. The one in the doorway ran out of power without ever hitting anything he intended to.

He was no coward, though. He threw his weapon at me as I passed him, and looked as though he might just come after me bare-handed. I took time to stun him, which gave the retreating woman time to fire into my human shield a couple more times. Burning people don't smell very good at all. And this one was liberally splattered with acrid sealant. Still I held onto him till I finally got the woman cornered and was able to get a shot at her. She collapsed in midair and hung there, drifting.

I hadn't realized how much noise they were making till they were all stunned or dead. The corridor was suddenly so silent my ears rang. There was an awful pain in my leg, and a nagging ache in the arm that had got singed way back before I got lost in the maintenance tubes. My head hurt, mostly from the reek of sealant and burned flesh. I thought for a moment I was going to be sick, which can be downright dangerous in freefall.

Heroic types like the Skyrider are expected—by themselves if by no one else—to take laser wounds in their stride, so to speak. Besides, there wasn't time to be sick. I was in Unit One now. Somewhere in this unit I would find the terrorist leaders, and, I hoped, my cousin Michael. But only if I didn't let the terrorists find me first.

The one who had escaped would bring others after me. I had to get out of that corridor quickly. It wasn't until I reached for a floating laser somebody had dropped that I realized my left hand had taken a hit, too. The fingers were so badly burned I couldn't force them to close around the laser's handgrip. For a startled moment I kept trying, unable to understand why the weapon kept retreating from my attempts to catch it. Finally I drew back my hand, looked at it, and thought about being sick again. It hadn't even hurt till I looked at it.

No time for that. I holstered my stun gun and

caught the retreating laser in my right hand. The laser
hadn't got any sealant on it, and it hadn't been fired
enough to register on the power gauge. Since Belters
were forbidden by Earther laws to own lethal side
arms, most of us had very little experience in their
use. However, I'm the exception of a lot of rules. I
was a better shot with a laser than with a stun gun,
and the one I'd just acquired fit my hand like it was
made for me.

I left the casualties, and the rest of their weapons,
to drift where they would. If I hadn't let a wit-
ness escape, I might have tried to clean up the
scene and see if I could get the bodies draped on
handholds in a realistic fashion so no one would
know I'd been there, but there was no time for that
now.

Perhaps the gruesome remains from the battle would
be useful in their own way. If my reputation pre-
ceded me, as Jamin always said it would, this ought
to scare off the more nervous terrorists. Maybe I
should hang a sign over the slaughterhouse scene:
The Skyrider Was Here.

I shook my head; shock made my mind fuzzy, and
there wasn't time for that, either. In fact, I was
rapidly running out of time for anything at all. I
couldn't possibly search the whole unit for Michael
before the guard who suffered sealant phobia returned with reinforcements. The place would soon be
swarming with terrorists, all looking for me. And this
time, they'd know I was there, in that unit. I had to
take control of the situation somehow. The logical
place to do that seemed to be the main control room.
If I couldn't find Michael, maybe I could make the
terrorists find him for me.

I hadn't set out originally to subdue the whole band of terrorists single-handed; but now that I thought of it, I might just as well. If I didn't, they would certainly subdue me.

CHAPTER THIRTEEN

Of course it wasn't quite as simple as that, and I wasn't quite fool enough to think it would be. As a matter of fact, I wasn't in any condition to do much thinking at all just then. Contrary to heroic expectations, even the Skyrider hurt when burned.

At first I thought I could just ignore it; but when I set out along the corridor in what I thought would be a straight glide, and crashed painfully against a wall not very far from where I'd started, I realized I wasn't ignoring it very well at all.

I had a standard first aid packet in my belt, but it didn't contain anything that would do much good for laser burns. The kit I carried was put together by Belters, for Belters, and it contained everything one might need for a lot of scraped knuckles and black eyes. It also contained some very effective painkillers, since we've been known to break each other's bones from time to time, but I hadn't liked to use them. They tended to cloud one's judgment.

So, of course, did pain. I wasn't alone in the corridor any longer. I hadn't seen them coming, but there were terrorists collecting in a nasty little cluster several meters away from me, waiting to see what I would do. If they'd had any damn sense, they'd have blasted me before I saw them. Since they were Earthers, they surely hadn't any quaintly sentimental notion about making sure I was the enemy before they killed me. Besides, who else would I be, in that corridor at that time, with the bodies of the cannon fodder floating at the junction behind me?

They were amateurs. I kept surviving just because the people I was up against hadn't ever been in a real fight before. It wasn't that they wanted to make sure who I was before they killed me; it was that they weren't sure what to do about me at all. Maybe they'd never killed anybody before. Even Earthers must start out half human, with a few of the normal human emotions like compassion and a sense of decency. I was a crippled wreck, clumsy with pain and half helpless. Experienced Earthers would have finished me off. Amateurs wondered whether that would be quite exactly fair.

Whoever told them life was going to be fair told them one hell of a lie. It got a few of them dead. I couldn't afford to be squeamish, myself, when I couldn't see straight or move quickly or even think clearly. They were an obstacle, so I shot at it. I did have sense enough left to duck into a handy chamber at the same time.

There were shouts, curses, and a few poorly aimed shots back at me; but by then I was inside the chamber and punching up the door lock mechanism. I didn't imagine that would hold them back for long, but it gave me time to get out the first aid kit and fumble for the painkillers. I had to put my laser in my belt to do it, since my left hand wasn't going to be doing any useful work any time soon. When I had thought I'd tackle the terrorists single-handed, the image had been all too literal.

I was in a big chamber, two levels deep, with a lot of noisy machinery in the middle and nobody to tend to it—I'd checked on that before I put away the laser. There was another door at the other level, nominally below me. Awkwardly, with only one working leg to kick with, I made my way toward it while I was fussing with the first aid kit. As a result of trying to do two things at once when I wasn't fit to do even one, I lost most of the kit; but I did manage to hold onto the hypospray for pain.

It didn't give me back the use of either my hand or my leg, but it made me not mind either loss nearly as much. I didn't mind the loss of the remainder of the first aid kit, either. In fact, I didn't mind much of anything. I felt downright jolly. I even had a tendency to giggle.

Modern medicine is a wonderful thing. Maybe a little too wonderful, sometimes. Well, I'd known the risk of using the painkiller, and I'd done it anyway. I wouldn't have got far without it. Now the question was how far I could get *with* it. And the first step was to master the urge to giggle.

The terrorists curbed the tendency for me. They weren't even trying to figure out the lock on the door at their level. They were going to laser it open. I dropped the hypospray, drew my laser, and hung onto it while I punched out the opening sequence on the door at my level. It hadn't occurred to me that it might be locked from the outside, and luckily it wasn't. I suppose I could have lasered through it, but I didn't want to waste the time, the laser power, or the element of surprise, if there were more terrorists on the other side of it.

There were. There were at least a dozen of them, just going about their business in an ordinary way. Only two of them were anywhere near me, and only those two looked up when I came barging out of the machine chamber toward them. I stared right back at them while I locked the door behind me. Neither was carrying a riot gun. Both were armed with lasers, but so was I; and mine was drawn.

It would have been simple enough to shoot them both where they floated, and maybe I should have. If I'd had the stun gun out, instead of the laser, I probably would have. But that would have called us to the attention of everyone else in the corridor, and I didn't really want to do that.

Taking the two of them hostage, in the hope that their warm bodies would provide cover for me, was obviously useless. I'd seen what these people thought of hostages. They were, after all, the same breed of humans who'd produced the C.I.D. It was hardly surprising that they were equally ruthless. Besides, the policy did work, however repellent I might find it: since I knew nobody would hesitate to shoot them to get at me, I wasn't going to try to use them for shields.

However, there's one thing that the policy of counting any and all hostages expendable doesn't consider: the hostages themselves won't *feel* expendable. And if they know that their friends will shoot them without hesitation, but that their captor won't as long as they cooperate, they're really more likely to cooperate than not.

The two in front of me were a man and a woman,

both in Belter costume, same like mine. The woman
started to reach for her weapon, and thought better of
it just in time. I saw them figuring it out. If they
called attention to me, they were dead. If I took a
dislike to them for any reason, they were dead. But if
I didn't, they might live long enough to find some
means of overpowering me. Most people are fond of
living. Even Earthers. They don't have much regard
for other people's lives, but they have a healthy
respect for their own.

I let them make the decision. The man was maybe
a little brighter than the woman. He didn't look it; he
had nasty little animal eyes, too close together, and a
face that had never been wrinkled up with extraneous
expressions like laughter. But he had the whole situation figured out while the woman was still thinking
about her holstered laser.

She didn't think about it very long. Unlike her
companion, she knew how to smile; and she wasn't
too proud to do it when she finally figured out that
was the sensible response to the situation. She looked
right at me, let her hands float easily away from her
laser, and smiled. "Can we help you?" Her voice
was well modulated, her accent impeccable Company
English. She wasn't trying to signal anybody, or to
pretend she was anything she wasn't. We two, her
smile said, were so much smarter than the rest of
these folks, it wasn't even funny. We didn't have to
play any games with each other. We were too smart
for that.

It was, of course, a game. Behind her pretty,
innocent, warm brown eyes, I could almost see the
calculations being run. It hadn't escaped her attention
that I was badly wounded, and it didn't take a genius
to figure out how I could keep functioning in that

state. Drugs will put anybody's reaction time off. She was calculating mine.

I didn't see any reason to spoil her fun just yet. "Yes, please," I said. "I'd like an escort to the main control room. If you two will just kindly act like you're friends of mine, we might all live till we get there."

She thought she saw an opening. "Certainly. This way."

I shook my head. "I thought you looked smarter than that, I really did," I said.

I can't say what she saw in my eyes. I wasn't particularly trying to look dangerous; the situation by itself was enough danger for most people; but I wasn't feeling very patient or charitable, either. Anyway, she saw something she didn't like at all. Her face paled. She tried to smile again, but it wasn't as successful this time. "I thought it was worth a try," she said honestly. She was scared now, but she wasn't ashamed of it, and she wasn't going to whine about it. "You must be the Skyrider we've all heard so much about."

I gave her that much. It couldn't hurt me, and Michael might be right; the legend might actually help. "I'm the Skyrider." Her eyes widened just perceptibly. The name impressed her. And she hadn't quite believed it, till I said it.

The people down the corridor were beginning to wonder about us. I did have my weapon drawn, and while it wasn't directly aimed at either of these people—I don't like to aim a weapon till I know I'm going to fire it—it wasn't exactly aimed away from them, either.

Laser wounds don't bleed much, as a rule, but they're noticeable if you're looking; and the one on my thigh had played hell with my costume. If I had to, I could explain my appearance by saying I'd tangled with the Skyrider; but I wasn't sure these two would back me up, and I didn't feel like chatting with terrorists anyway.

"I really don't want to kill you," I said conversationally. "But your friends are getting curious."

At least they didn't resort to the usual indignant protests about what I could or couldn't do and/or expect to get away with. I half expected it from the man, who had been remarkably quiet so far, but who was watching me with the alert animal intelligence of a predator waiting for a chance to strike. But he only said, "This way," and gestured in the correct direction for the control room.

The woman glanced at him, controlled a look of puzzled disgust at his meekness, and tried without success to look as meek as he sounded.

They had every intention of tackling me at the first opportunity, of course. I'd have been suspicious if they hadn't. But for now, they were willing to pretend obedience, and I was willing to pretend I believed it. When we all three turned casually and wandered together along the corridor toward the main control room, our audience lost interest. I hadn't put my weapon away; but anybody who noticed that might also notice my physical condition, and figure I was just too generally upset to remember my manners.

I suppose the two I'd commandeered as an escort were hoping I was upset, too. It would mean I'd be more likely to give them an opening. If that was what they were waiting for, they didn't get it. We had to pass another cluster of terrorists. There seemed to be a lot of little groups of them around, gathered for no apparent reason unless they really were trading recipes or discussing the price of stun guns in the Belt or something. I was surprised by the sheer number of them, but it didn't alarm me. Like I said, they were amateurs. Why else would they have been clustered around in useless little groups like that, doing nothing, when there were intruders aboard and two great hostile fleets facing off outside?

Anyway, my two didn't make any effort to use the group as we passed, because I got right up near them as we approached the others, and it was pretty obvious that they might be able to stop me, or the group might, but that I would get the two I was with. They weren't gung-ho enough to be willing to sacrifice their lives in the effort to kill me, though they'd have sacrificed somebody else's life if they saw the chance.

It helped that we all knew the prevalent attitude toward human shields and hostages. If my two called attention to me, I might not even get a chance to shoot them; their compatriots might do it for me. They kept quiet, and we floated, unchallenged, on our way.

They thought they'd finally found their chance when we came upon a rack of sealant bottles in an empty corridor. There was nobody handy to shoot the couple I'd commandeered except me, and I'd have to be damned quick and steady to get both before they could disable my weapon. Actually, it was a clever move for people as inexperienced at this sort of thing as those two were. It could have succeeded; most people wouldn't have recognized a bottle of sealant as a potential weapon. If I hadn't so recently used it that way myself, I might not even have noticed it.

CHAPTER FOURTEEN

The corridor hummed with muted engine sounds. We were nearing the master control chamber, and I suppose the ruling class thought they were well enough protected by the swarms of terrorists everywhere else, so they didn't need any of them cluttering up the inner sanctum corridors. High muckymucks are very much alike, whether they're Earthers or terrorists or little green men from a distant solar system: they think so well of themselves that they can't comfortably consort with their hirelings for fear they'll be contaminated by the ordinary.

At least, that's my conclusion after watching how they behave, and this crowd hadn't done anything yet to change my opinion. The odd thing is that people who rank below the muckymucks, in a well run organization that treats everybody fairly decently, tend to agree with the muckymucks' opinion. They'll go to startling lengths to keep the ordinary from sullying their masters.

We hadn't got that near the control center yet, so I didn't know how the two I was with were going to react when it came down to a choice between their lives and peril to their leaders. They didn't take any risks at all till we were quite alone, and then they weren't hard to discourage.

I'd had my eye on the sealant rack since we came in sight of it. I saw them recognize its potential. They weren't obvious about it, but they were a little scared of what they were going to do, and it showed. But it didn't stop them. The nearer we got to the sealant, the farther apart the two of them floated. It was very casual, done without so much as a glance at me. I guess I was supposed to think air currents just happened to drift them toward opposite walls.

I let myself lag farther and farther behind them. I could have closed the distance, instead, and stopped their attempt before it was properly started, but I wanted to see how they would handle it. They should have kept better track of me; but they were so afraid I'd notice what they were planning, they were afraid to look at me at all.

That was the only real mistake they made. When they came level with the rack of sealant bottles, they both moved as smoothly as if the whole routine had been choreographed. If they'd kept better track of me, it might have worked. The man grabbed up a sealant bottle and inverted it while the woman braced herself against a freefall handhold on the opposite wall and drew her laser. Sealant sprayed all over the center of the corridor where I was supposed to be, and the woman's laser covered it nicely, ready for me to emerge from the gray gunk. But I wasn't there.

It took them a moment to figure it out. The man looked bewildered, then angry. The woman just looked angry. She couldn't find a target. The sealant hadn't hit anything except walls. I'd taken refuge in a doorway far enough back from them to avoid most of the mess, and to be hidden from the laser as long as I kept well back against the inset door. "Nice try," I said.

They saw me, then, and the man dropped the sealant and reached for his laser. The woman used hers, but she couldn't get an angle on me. I had mine braced on a handhold, and I'd known not only what the target would be, but roughly where. The man's laser burned his fingers when the light from mine hit it, and he let it go with a strangled cry of rage.

The woman fired again, uselessly.

"Put it away," I said. "I still don't want to kill you."

Reluctantly, she put her laser away. The two of them waited while I kicked away from the doorway and joined them again. The man's hand pained him, but he was too angry to let it show any more than he could help. The woman hadn't got hurt anywhere but in her pride; but then, that can be the most dangerous place to hit an amateur.

"If you ever have to try that again," I said, "watch to see whether your victim sees it coming. That was the only real mistake you made."

The woman glared at me resentfully; she didn't want my advice. But the man blinked his little piggy eyes in surprise and said, "I didn't like to look back, in case that would alert you."

"It's natural to look back now and then when someone's following you with a drawn laser," I said.

"What are you going to do now?" the woman asked.

I looked at her. "Do? I'm going to do what I

intended to do all along. I'm going to rescue my cousin Michael." I hesitated. "Look, I wonder whether you two could satisfy a little curiosity? I mean, I thought when I came out here that I'd be dealing with a couple dozen terrorists, at the most. But there must be a hundred of you, or more. And well armed, all of you. What the hell is going on?"

"Earth must be taught a lesson," said the woman. Her voice had the pedantic, flat tone of a fanatic—or a poor liar. "They can't continue to oppress the Colonial masses—"

I must have made a gesture of some kind, though I wasn't aware of it. She shut up. I admit to a fleeting moment of rage when she spoke; my hand hurt, my leg hurt, my head hurt, I hadn't yet found Michael, the two fleets outside might start a shooting war at any moment with us in the middle, and this dirt dweller wanted to play games.

"We're government agents," said the man. "You don't need the name of the agency. I think you know its purpose."

"To start a war. And give the public the impression that Earth wasn't the aggressor," I said. "Is the C.I.D. in on this? Is that why they let me make the rescue?"

"Egan," said the woman, glaring at the man. "That's classified information. What do you think you're doing, telling her—"

Egan simply smiled. "She'll never get off the station." He transferred the smile to me. It wasn't a pleasant smile. "And if you did, who'd believe you?"

"A whole damn agency for the purpose," I said. "I might have guessed. In fact, I should have guessed. Damn. All right, folks. Let's move along."

"You'll never get away with this," said the woman.

"I've heard that line somewhere before," I said.

"You can't seriously hope to—"

"Do me a favor," I said. "Don't tell me what I can or can't seriously hope. And stop trying to distract me with chatter. I asked a question and I got an answer. Now shut up and keep moving."

She shut up and we kept moving. I stayed well behind, where they couldn't see me without turning their heads, but near enough that I wouldn't have any trouble killing them quickly if the need arose. If they got a good look at me, the need just might arise; the painkiller I'd used was wearing off, and it probably showed. It was only meant to last long enough for a person to get to Sick Bay, and that wasn't expected to be a long journey. If these two realized that, they might think they'd gotten another opening.

And I really didn't want to kill them. Not because I had any particular affection for either of them; in fact, I didn't like them much at all. But in general, the idea of killing people is at least moderately repellent to me. It's so irrevocable. I've done it, and will again; but I don't like it.

I thought they would make another try at stopping me before we reached the master control chamber, but they didn't. They never saw an opening, and they weren't quite good enough to make one. They didn't get to kill me, and I didn't have to kill them. We arrived at the control chamber intact and angry.

At least, they looked angry, with me and with themselves. And I felt angry, with the whole damn situation. Earth had set up an entire, Company-funded agency for the purpose of starting a war without looking guilty. Not that it came as a complete surprise: I had half suspected it, but I'd hoped the suspicion was paranoid. I wasn't happy to have it confirmed.

I made the two terrorist agents enter the chamber ahead of me. They didn't like that. But they didn't have any choice in the matter. In their place, I wouldn't have liked it, either; it was a hell of a place to be. If I didn't kill them, their own superiors probably would. They went in low and cautious, and I could see them tensing, getting ready to dive out of the way if anybody fired.

Nobody did. The first person I saw inside was Michael, strapped to a wall at the back of the chamber, away from the control consoles. I grinned at him, but he didn't grin back. They hadn't been treating him well at all. He looked as though the effort to smile might hurt.

However, he also looked, at last, like the warrior I had expected when I brought him along. The boyish look was gone, and some of the civilization. His hooded eyes watched me. The grim set of his face betrayed nothing. The apparent relaxation of his body, limp and helpless against his bonds, concealed a poised readiness that would be deadly if he saw the smallest opportunity for rebellion. Since the Incident, he had become a man of peace, marrying and raising babies and becoming gentle in his ways. Now the gentleness was stripped away. This man would require less rescuing. Which was as well, since I wasn't quite as fit for the task as when I set out to do it.

There were two guards with Michael, both of whom just looked at the three of us when we entered. I thought at first that it hadn't quite registered with them what we were. As it turned out, they knew before we got there, but I didn't know that.

At the control consoles there were several computer operators, and three Earther officers who didn't bother to masquerade as Colonials or terrorists. They wore Earth Fighter uniforms. They also wore happy, expectant smiles that would have puzzled me, since they seemed to be directed at me, but I'd heard the chamber door across the corridor snick open just as I swung in through the door to this chamber, so I knew what they were really smiling at.

Maybe I could have avoided capture, even then. If I had kicked straight across the room, into reach of one of those EF officers, I'd have had a hostage they might not have considered expendable. I even had one selected for the job: the one who was looking at me, instead of at the unseen agents at my back. He had Michael's personal Comm hooked over one finger, dangling it mockingly in my sight, just to let me know exactly where I'd gone wrong, and by how great a margin.

Overconfident hotshot Skyrider does it again. These calm EF officers must have got their jollies while they listened to me fight my way to them, when all the while they were planning on my arrival and making arrangements to stop me at the door.

The Comm was voice-activated, and I'd had mine set on the intercom frequency anyway. All they had to do was listen to my various battles along the way to know how near I was getting and how soon I'd arrive. No wonder the corridor outside was deserted when we came through. They wouldn't want anybody to spoil their fun at the last minute; if I got that far, they wanted me to come all the way in, so they could show me just how stupid and futile the whole effort had been.

Maybe they even hoped I would go for the guy

with Michael's personal Comm on his finger. I'd got this far: maybe they wanted to watch me killed before their very eyes. But I was just too damn tired and disgusted to bother. If they wanted to kill me, they'd have to do it unprovoked. I knew I couldn't move fast enough to get them all, and there was no guarantee they wouldn't consider even their EF officers expendable. I didn't wait for them to spell it out for me. I just handed my laser to Egan and waited.

"The stun gun, too," said an officer. The ones behind me were close, now; one of them pressed a laser against my back. That was a stupid move. Lasers are meant to be used at a distance. They work well enough, up close; but if you move in close enough for your target to feel the barrel, you're also close enough for your target to knock it aside and take it away from you with a reasonable chance of success. Either they were even clumsier than I'd come to expect, or they were testing, at considerable risk to themselves, the ease with which I'd allowed myself to be caught.

I said, hoping my tone sounded properly defeated, "Sorry. I forgot I had it." I moved my arm out of the way so the laser bearer behind me could take my stun gun out of its holster.

One of the officers smiled at me with what might have been genuine sympathy. "How unfortunate that you should come all this way, only to be overwhelmed almost at the moment of triumph."

I shrugged, and immediately regretted it; my burned hand brushed against something, and the painkiller had definitely worn off. I pulled it protectively back against my body and let my face show the pain. It was time to stop looking competent. They already thought I wasn't, and I didn't want to disabuse them of the notion, yet. The more they underestimated me, the better.

"Everybody makes mistakes," I said, letting my voice catch a little as I jarred my hand again, then caught the wrist in my good hand, to hold it steady. "I should have remembered the personal Comms. I should have known you'd have his."

The two behind me hustled me on into the room, and hustled my erstwhile hostages out past me. The woman glared in triumph as she went. The man just looked at me. I couldn't read anything at all in his piggy little eyes.

The EF with Michael's personal Comm gave it back to him, I'm not sure why. Maybe it was a gesture, to show how little they thought of our potential as adversaries. If so, that was good; they wouldn't be on guard against us if we did find an opening.

But I wasn't really paying much attention. Everything kept going in and out of focus, like a cheap holofilm, and since my best defense now was complete helplessness, I didn't really fight it.

"So this is the great Skyrider," said someone. The voice seemed to come from a distance, past howling winds.

I blinked stupidly around the room, trying to look vaguely stubborn and defeated.

"Not so very great, after all," someone said. He sounded almost disappointed.

I had let myself relax, slowly, giving the appearance of a person at the outside limit of her endurance, clinging grimly to consciousness. Now I made a last valiant effort to retain some dignity—at least, I hoped that was what it would look like—and blinked owlishly at the EFs, obviously unable to single out the one who had spoken. It was time to trot out some of the hoary old indignant claptrap my hostages had tried on me.

"You can't expect to get away with this." I was ignoring the personal insult, about how great the Skyrider wasn't; in the time-honored tradition of the self-righteous, I was concentrating on the magnitude of their affront to the dignity of Right Actions or decency or the spirit of Honorable Warfare, or some damn thing. . . . I admit, I was a little vague on the details, never having been big on fairness and honor myself. The idea was to convince them of my helplessness and confusion, so they wouldn't pay attention to what I really had to say.

"We'll get away with it, all right," said somebody.

I really was running out of strength and finding it hard to concentrate. But if I didn't get the wording right, they might cut me off too soon, or Jamin might not understand what I wanted. And now that I'd remembered the damn personal Comms, I wanted to get some use out of them.

"You think you've won," I said dizzily. "But Jamin . . . Jamin got the hostages away from you. . . . He'll take them . . ." The chamber was fading out of focus again. The dizzy helplessness wasn't an act anymore. "He'll have, the *Defiance* will have recorded . . . from the intercom frequency . . . Jamin, get out, get it to Board Advisor—"

Somebody hit me. At least, I think that's what happened. But I was pretty far gone by then anyway. Maybe I just lost the fight for consciousness. I heard somebody say, "Get a med-tech," and somebody else say, "Why bother?" It didn't really matter to me, at the time.

CHAPTER FIFTEEN

When I woke, their med-techs had been at me. If they hadn't, I suppose I wouldn't have woken at all; the burns I'd sustained wouldn't have proved fatal in themselves, but the shock would have done. I suppose that's why they bothered. They probably weren't quite sure yet what to do with me, but hostages of any sort are usually of greater value alive than dead.

They hadn't taken the trouble to mend me completely. That, if it ever got done, would take more time than they had available to them now. My left leg from hip to ankle had been fastened into an immobilizing brace, which was actually rather decent of them, considering that for their purposes they could have done as well with a spray of burn plaster and some extra painkiller. This way, if I moved around, I wouldn't do the thigh muscles any more damage than they'd already been done.

My left hand was more of a problem, and they'd solved it the easy way: burn plaster and painkillers.

There wasn't really much else they could have done. It was badly charred, and would eventually have to be rebuilt, if I lived that long. Meantime, the burn plaster soothed and protected it about as well as anything could, outside of Sick Bay.

Michael was beside me, patiently waiting while I assessed the damages. We weren't in the control chamber anymore. And he wasn't strapped to a wall, as he had been when I first found him. Apparently they thought the lock on whatever chamber we were in would be adequate restraint. They might even be right. We weren't in any condition to put up much of a fight against anything, not even a lock.

The med-techs had been at Michael, too. He had burn plaster on both arms and the side of his head, and he looked as though they'd skimped on the pain-killers. His face was drawn and white, with sunken blue areas like bruises around his eyes, which nonetheless retained the look of controlled menace that made him look so much less like a freckle-faced boy. "Sleeping beauty awakes." His tone was light, and he even attempted a smile, but it wasn't at all convincing.

"Where are we?" I asked, peering at the empty chamber around us.

"That's classic," he said. "Couldn't you ask something more original?"

I looked at him. "Don't be snide, Michael. If something's bothering you, just say it, so we can deal with it and get on to figuring out what to do next."

"Sure. A plan for every situation. What do you pull out of your helmet for 'Taken Hostage by Terrorists'? I'd really like to know." He was trying to sound angry, and maybe he even was angry; but there were shadows in his eyes I didn't understand.

"I could tell you more easily if I knew exactly what the situation was."

"Oh, that's easy. Famous hotshot Skyrider plays into the War Agency's hands and gets herself captured when she's supposed to be rescuing hostages. *Voila*, they have new and better hostages. What the hell did you think you were doing, anyway?"

"Rescuing you."

"Some rescue." Unexpectedly, he grinned.

I didn't return it. I didn't feel like grinning. "You're right, I've seen better. And if you hadn't bought the damn Skyrider image wholesale, maybe you'd be able to see that we'd be better off doing something about the mess we're in, instead of complaining about how we got here. For that matter, how did you get here?"

"The same way you got here: War, Incorporated, brought me. In the person of several of its agents, a.k.a. terrorists. Much against my will."

"I meant how did they catch you in the first place?"

"Oh, that." He looked away from me for the first time, shrugged, and met my gaze again. "It's a long story. Couldn't we skip that part?" A hint of the boy's sheepish grin showed in the warrior's wolfish eyes.

"Sure, if we also skip the part about how the famous Skyrider isn't quite the hotshot miracle worker you thought she was. I warned you I wouldn't necessarily live up to the image."

"And I told you it would be valuable anyway. Well, maybe it would have been—if you hadn't got so involved in playing the part that you thought you were invulnerable. Do you really have a plan for getting out of here?''

"How can I? You still haven't told me where 'here' is."

"We're in a chamber just off the main control chamber. The charts called it a briefing room."

"Did it have a letter code?"

He told me it, which placed it in my memory of the blueprints. We were exactly adjacent to the control chamber, on the side toward Unit Four, which was the unit full of storage chambers where I'd found the hostages. Beyond Unit Four was the flight deck, on Unit Six. Since I sincerely hoped that Jamin had departed the station, I didn't see any other way for us to get clear away than by requisitioning a terrorist agency shuttle, and I said so.

"Sure, no problem," he said. "All we have to do is escape a locked chamber, travel unnoticed through half of Unit One and all of Unit Four—" He was laughing at me, silently. I couldn't think why.

"Can't you think on the bright side of anything?"

"What bright side?" That wolfish grin again.

It was a valid point: I couldn't think of a bright side, either. Our location could have been worse, of course. So could our health. We could have been dead. "I don't know. But it won't do us any good to count up the disadvantages, anyway," I said crossly.

"At least we'll know what we're up against."

"I already have a pretty good idea what we're up against." While we talked, I had been looking around the chamber. There was a door on the side toward the control chamber, but I didn't waste any time on it; there's an old saying about frying pans and fires that would have applied if we could have got through that door.

However, as Michael silently pointed out, there was something much more interesting on the wall opposite the door: an entrance to the maintenance tubes. It wasn't locked. I moved away from it disinterestedly. At least, I hoped I didn't look interested. "I suppose they're watching us?" I asked.

He gestured toward a surveillance camera above the door to the control chamber. "They were. I put it out of action, first thing."

"And they didn't do anything about it?"

"Well, they got a little agitated, but they didn't replace it and they didn't move us." He rubbed his chin ruefully, and I saw the blue hint of a bruise there. "They weren't happy about it, though."

"Why did you bother? Did you have a plan you haven't mentioned?"

"No. I just didn't like being watched." He moved purposefully to the maintenance tube and looked back at me expectantly.

"Of course they're still listening," I said.

"I suppose so. I doubt if the mike I found was the only one they had."

"You put a microphone out of action, too?" When he nodded, I smiled. "My, haven't we been busy."

"It was something to do."

"Well, let's hope the mike you found *was* the only one they had, because otherwise they now know what our plan is."

"What plan?" He stared, startled, from the maintenance tube to me and then around the room, obviously wondering whether he'd missed something, or whether I was dumb enough to be about to mention the tubes out loud.

"The one about stealing a shuttle, you remember."

"Oh. You call that a plan?"

I ignored that. "D'you have any idea what they're saving us for?"

"Sure. We replace the hostages Jamin got away with." He had the hatch open now, and was waiting for me to join him beside it.

"How d'you know he did get away with them?" I tried to sound defeated and weary. It wasn't difficult; I felt defeated and weary. I didn't want to go back into those claustrophobic tunnels, and I didn't see how Michael could fit into them at all.

"Public news announced it while you were getting your beauty rest. He had a little trouble with the war fleets outside, but considering his cargo, they finally let him go. I gather he's taken the hostages in to an orbit nearer Earth, where they can all be reunited with their happy friends and families. I don't know why the C.I.D. hasn't blasted us yet." He gestured impatiently toward the tube.

"Why would they? They never wanted to in the first place: this isn't a terrorist station, it's a government agency. The same government that gave us the C.I.D. I suppose they'll claim the terrorists fled, so nobody'll ever have to blast their nice station." I took the Comm unit from behind my ear; that was probably how they were listening, same like before.

"How could they have fled, with the whole Colonial Fleet outside? Wouldn't they have been stopped, or at least reported?"

"Of course not. They fled before the Earthers got here, and the Colonials let them go. Don't forget the Colonials are supposedly behind all this."

"Well, if the terrorists are gone, who's holding us?"

"Don't confuse me with facts. Beside, the story only has to account for a few terrorists. They'll go on hiding the greater part of their agency on Station Newhome. They still have a war to start, after all."

· "Meantime, maybe we had better make that plan you mentioned." He looked meaningfully at the tube; he was getting impatient, but I had wanted to be sure the so-called terrorists weren't going to come charging in to stop us when they heard him open the hatch. Since they hadn't arrived yet, I decided they weren't coming, and joined him beside the hatch.

"That's easy," I said, holding my Comm unit up for him to see. "I thought we might tackle the next ones to come through that door, and just batter our way out. Or is that too risky for you?"

Frowning, he took off his personal Comm and looked at me. He wanted to say we might need them. His eyes said it. Aloud, all he said was, "I'd rather wait for a chance that *is* a chance. They'd kill us."

"They probably will, anyway." I wondered how he would propel himself along a tunnel that would be all but skin tight for him; and whether he remembered the layout well enough to find his way through it to Unit Six—or to any other exit.

"Maybe not, if we go along with them till we see a real opening." At my gesture, he handed me his Comm and slid headfirst into the tube. In gravity, he couldn't have done it at all, but in freefall it looked much simpler than I had expected.

"They may not give us a real opening," I said aloud to the empty room. "It's just my luck to be stuck here with a damn coward Martian. Well, if we're not going to do anything, then just shut up and let me sleep. I don't feel good." I let the Comm units float away from me and joined him in the tube, hooking my good foot over the handle to close the hatch cover after us.

When the light from behind us was blocked by the
closing cover, I damn near panicked. I'd had enough
of these cramped, blind tunnels. I darted forward,
and banged up against Michael's feet. He said,
"Steady," and waited a moment. "You okay,
hotshot?"

"Just great," I said crossly. Our voices echoed
down the smooth black distance before us. "If we
get out of this alive, I absolutely will not ever so
much as *look* at another maintenance tube. I spent
half a lifetime in these already, looking for you. I
don't suppose you happen to know your way or
anything lucky like that?"

He chuckled. It was a dry, whispery sound in the
enclosed, stale darkness. "I know my way. Earthers
boarded this station twice, during the war, before we
got the defense systems set up to repel them. They
thought the place was haunted. No Colonial Warriors
in evidence, and yet the Earthers kept dying. In most
mysterious ways."

"I'll bet they did. D'you think you can arrange it
so we don't do the same?"

"I know I can. Whatsamatta you, big brave Skyrider
afraid of the dark?"

"You damn betcha. This place gives me the creeps.
How in space can you move so fast? If anybody'd
asked, I'd have sworn you were too big to fit in here
at all."

"I've had a lot of practice. And don't complain
about the size of the tubes: that's what will keep the
Earthers out of here. I hope. How's the leg?"

"It's okay. They must have given me enough
painkiller to make a rock silly. But I do wish I had
two working hands."

"I'd settle for one fully functional arm."

"How bad are those burns? I didn't notice you had them when I first found you."

He hesitated. "I didn't."

"You what!"

That papery chuckle again, eerie and haunted, echoing down the unending tunnel. "I thought they'd killed you."

"Oh." I thought about it. "Oh. Brave last stand?"

"Something like that. Remember when you were on Earth, right after that, um, your accident?"

"Right after I killed my lover through sheer stupidity and neglect, you mean?"

"I understood it was a clogged air filter on a shuttle run."

"If that ain't stupidity and neglect, what is?"

"Okay. Anyway. You talked about what you called the Colonial Incident."

"Sure." I mimicked my tone at the time: "I know they called it a war on Mars."

"Well, I got the impression then—oops, sorry." He'd kicked me in the face; this wasn't the easiest mode of travel, nor the most comfortable place for conversation, that I'd ever seen. "You okay?"

"Sure. Just a few broken teeth, I think."

"Well, that's about standard for a friendly conversation among Belters, the way I hear it."

"Leave off the ethnic slurs and tell your story, or whatever it was you were going to tell me."

"Sure." He moved forward more cautiously, trying not to kick me again. "Well. Maybe I was wrong, but I kind of got the impression you were sorry you missed the last war."

"Not sorry, exactly." He didn't say anything, and we moved forward in silence for a while. "I guess I felt guilty. I guess I had some damnfool notion that war was some kind of proving ground, or something. You know?''

"I know." His voice came back to me, dry and sad in the stifling darkness. "Isn't that why you've built that hotshot Skyrider image? Trying to prove something?"

In that enclosed space, I could hardly hit him. "What the hell? Go practice psych-tending on somebody else."

"Sorry. I only meant . . . Well, I'd have felt . . . I wouldn't have liked it if you'd died, if they'd killed you, because you're still trying to prove you're as . . . tough, or whatever . . . as I am. You know, because I was in the war."

"Jeez. Remind me, if we ever get out of here, to knock your teeth in, okay?"

"Would you rather I didn't mind if they killed you?" He sounded genuinely surprised and puzzled.

"Are all Martians as stupid as you? Strike that: how would you know? No, dear cousin, I wouldn't rather you didn't mind if somebody killed me. What I mind is your space happy Martian ego."

"Oh." He thought about it for a while, and figured it out. "Well, I didn't mean I wouldn't mind about you, personally . . ."

"Forget it, Brave Leader. Just concentrate on getting us out of here. If you really can."

CHAPTER SIXTEEN

He really could. Or anyway, he knew the way. We had a bad moment or two, but they weren't his fault. He traveled as easily in the tubes as if he could see where we were going, and he seemed to know where every junction was and which of the tunnels went our way, though without his help I wouldn't necessarily even have known there were choices to make.

Unfortunately, not all the junctions curved as gradually as those I'd negotiated when I was in the tunnels by myself. And with that whacking great brace on my leg, I wasn't as agile as I could have wished. The ninety-degree turns were tight, but I managed them. Then we came on one that was more like forty-five degrees.

He said, "Turn coming up."

I said. "Okay," and stuck out my good hand against one wall and my forearm against the opposite one, to slow my forward progress. Ahead of me, Michael bumped hard against something, which bounced him back against me before he could stop himself. He cursed, muttered, edged forward again, and banged into something else, this time controlling the rebound so I didn't get feet in my face. From the rustles and scratching sounds he then made, I knew we were coming up on something I wouldn't like. "Does the tunnel narrow, or what?" I don't think I sounded any more anxious than I felt. That was ample.

"Mostly what." His voice was muffled, and he sounded out of breath. Then the rustlings and scratchings stopped, and when I reached ahead of me in the tunnel I couldn't find his feet; only a wall.

"Another damn ninety-degree turn?"

His voice came back to me, muffled and breathless: "I'm afraid it's worse than that. More like forty-five degrees. I'd forgotten this. It's the junction between two units; when we get through here, we'll be in Unit Four, and from there it's clear sailing to Unit One."

My eyes ached from trying to see in the darkness. I moved forward cautiously to investigate the turn. "Forty-five degrees? Hell, it feels like one hundred eighty. How in space am I supposed to get around that?" I floated forward, into the turn, till the top half of my body was in the other tunnel. Even with two working legs, that wouldn't have been the way to do it; legs don't bend frontward, and there wasn't room to pull them through straight.

"You have to turn your back to the curve," he said. "Then your legs can bend around it as you come through."

"Right. I figured out that much." From the more or less seated position I was in now, bent forward at the waist with my head in one tunnel and my feet in the other, I could almost reach back to feel the brace on my leg. In fact, I could feel the top of it. And I thought I could probably manage to release the fastenings there. But I couldn't reach the additional straps at knee and ankle, and I didn't think I could squirm out of it without unfastening those. "I don't think it's going to work."

"There's just barely room," he said. "It isn't comfortable, but you can do it."

"I'm not so sure about that." I slid back out of the curve, squirmed awkwardly around till I thought I was turned over relative to the curve, and moved forward again. This time it was at my back, as intended. And as Michael had said, with some effort, my back would bend that far. My leg wouldn't.

"I forgot the leg brace," he said.

"I thought you had." For a moment I couldn't move in either direction, and had to fight down panic; then I got the brace free so I could slip back the way I had come. I tried it again, the other side up. And got stuck in a different place, but I was just as stuck. "I can't get it around this damn corner, and I can't reach to get it off," I said.

"Can you reach the top straps?"

"Only just."

"If you unfasten them, can you wiggle out of it?"

"I don't think so. I'll try." I moved back into the curve, to the point where I could reach the straps, and unfastened them. It wasn't that easy, of course, particularly with only one hand, but eventually I got it done. Then I slid forward, not quite cautiously enough. The damn brace caught even sooner than before. The knee and ankle straps held, and the brace stayed where it was while I tried to go forward. The thigh muscles—what was left of them—protested. I think I yelled.

Michael couldn't reach me, of course, except with his feet, which wasn't much comfort. I don't know whether I'd have really noticed if he could have done better; despite the liberal dose of painkiller I'd been given, about all I could clearly perceive was pain.

Somebody was whimpering. Somebody else was saying my name. When I got the two sounds sorted out, I stopped the one and answered the other.

"What happened?" he asked.

"I got the damn brace hung up at the corner." My voice sounded thin and small, like a frightened child or a very old woman. "Isn't there any other way into Unit Four?"

"None that doesn't involve a sharp turn. Can't you get the brace off?"

"If I could, I would have done, by now," I said crossly. "Oh, I'm sorry. It's not your fault. Damn. I'm half scared to move, it hurts so much. Wait a minute, I'll try going back and turning over again." But that didn't work, either. No matter which side up I was when I tackled the corner, the leg or the brace or both got hung up, and I couldn't get them through.

I don't know whether it would have been any better if I'd been able to see. It wouldn't have helped me get around the turn, but I might not have felt so horribly enclosed, so crowded by the hard, invisible walls and the stale, motionless air. The mass of the whole station seemed to press in on that corner, conspiring with the awkward metal and plastic contrivance strapped to my leg to keep me there, wedged in place, buried in darkness. . . .

After the third attempt to force my way around the cramped, unyielding corner, I gave up. I just stopped where I was when the brace got jammed, and cursed. "It's no use. There's no way I can get the damn thing through here."

Michael quoted the old Belter maxim at me: " 'There is no problem that can't be solved through judicious application of brute force and ignorance.' "

"I've applied both, liberally," I said. "Where'd you hear that, anyway? I didn't know you'd spent any time in the Belt."

"We use brute force and ignorance on Mars, too. What's the brace made of, do you know?"

"Plastic, I guess, and some metal."

"You've tried bending it?"

"Of course. It doesn't bend."

"What's catching at the bottom? Your foot, or the brace?"

"Both. Mostly the brace, I guess. I think if I could bend that, my foot would bend enough to come through."

"Do you have anything you could use for leverage? If you put something between the brace and the wall, couldn't you lever the brace around the curve that way?"

"What did you have in mind? I ran right out of tools and weapons both, about the time I reached the control chamber."

"They didn't take your holster, did they, when they disarmed you?"

"No. And you're right: it's plasteel-backed. I'm ashamed to say I didn't even think of it." Reaching back with my good hand, I wrestled the thing off my belt and used it to lever the brace away from the wall. Progress after that was slow, but it was progress. I nearly broke my ankle at one point, and I did break the holster eventually, but I got through.

Michael helped, by hooking his toes under my arms and tugging me forward while I fought with the brace. Afterward, the brace was still in good enough condition to fasten back on, to protect my leg and, more important, to avoid catching the loose top end on anything and thus yanking my leg where the bottom straps that I couldn't reach were still fastened.

My holster was bent and twisted and useless, but I hadn't a weapon to put in it anyway. When I'd caught my breath I said, "I'll never go anywhere with you again. I'd always heard Martians were cheap dates, but this is ridiculous."

"Thrills, adventure, excitement," he said. "What more could you ask?" He sounded almost as weary as I felt.

"Life, liberty, and the pursuit of happiness." My voice sounded thin and distant, even to my own ears.

"Greedy wench."

"I told you I'm a mercenary. Greed is my middle name."

"I thought your middle name was Vandy."

"That's my other middle name." I sighed: a broken little whisper of air in the darkness. "Michael, look, I'm sorry, I really am, but I just can't go any farther."

"After all that, you'd give up? We're almost there. The tube through Unit Four is straight and easy, all the way." At least, I think that's what he said. I couldn't quite hear him; his voice seemed to fade and grow and fade again, and not all the words made sense. The struggle with that corner had taken all the strength I had.

"Sure, okay." It wasn't worth arguing. "Go ahead. I'll be right behind you." I meant it, too, but I didn't move. While I rested, the pain of the laser burns had dulled to a bearable level. If I moved, the charred and torn muscles would protest again. I thought of telling him that: explaining how comfortable I was, how much more sensible it would be for me to stay where I was, where I could rest and listen to the quiet thrum of the engines and smell the sweet damp tang of rocks and feel the warm, healing emanations from the lamp beside my bed. But I didn't have the strength to speak. I was sleepy, and anyway I'd forgotten what I meant to say, or to whom I'd been speaking, or why.

I thought lazily that I should turn out the lamp before I went to sleep. But maybe I'd look at my holograms from Earth, first. Earth was a pretty place. I liked the sky and clouds and green groundcover. While I'd been on Earth I'd never felt quite comfortable: it didn't seem safe to be so unprotected. The chamber was too big. Clouds were alien and strange, and water fell out of them sometimes; right out of the sky, getting all over everything underneath them. I wouldn't want to live on Earth, but it was pleasant to look at my holograms and remember. . . .

"Melacha!" Something jostled my shoulders. "Melacha, snap out of it. Come on. You can do it. Just a little farther."

I wasn't safe in my bed on Home Base. I opened my eyes, and the lamp wasn't there to be turned out. There were no holograms. Only darkness, spotted with dizzying red stars like tiny, silent explosions before my eyes. I remembered Michael and said dully, "Sure. I'm coming." I even put out my hand to give myself a little push forward. But the Gypsies distracted me with their song. It was one I'd never heard before.

Django had been one of the last few Gypsies in the Belt. He was one of the last few heroes in the

universe. He was my love. He had survived a lot of
hazards and a lot of battles in his time, and saved a
lot of people's lives on rescue missions nobody else
was brave or maybe dumb enough to make. He died
on my shuttle of a clogged air filter that I should
have checked before the flight. It blew its top, and it
crushed my skull, and it killed my love.

The med-techs had put a metal plate in my head to
hold my brains in, said I should be grateful they
didn't have to rebuild my pretty face, and turned me
loose to fly again, in a world that felt suddenly
desolate and empty, because Django wasn't in it
anymore.

It was after that accident that I first heard the
Gypsies singing. I had known there were ghosts among
the asteroids, but I'd never heard them before. At
first I thought they sang to haunt me, to taunt me, to
remind me how wrong I was to be alive when Django
was dead. That was nonsense, of course. When I'd
finally given myself permission to be alive, and more
or less forgiven myself for the death of my love, I
could hear their songs more clearly.

They were just singing to themselves. They sang
of stars, of space, of freedom; of solar winds and
asteroids; of dreams, and death, and life, and hope.
And sometimes, when I was lonely or needed help,
they sang for me.

On some level, I had always known they would
sing me to death, one day: not to kill me, but to
comfort me. If they could save me, they would sing
the help I needed; and they had done, several times
now. But if I was beyond their help, they would sing
for that.

I didn't fancy I would meet Django in some ala-
baster afterlife with wings and harps and golden char-

iots and pearly gates. I just knew that when the time came for me to die, the Gypsies wouldn't let me go down into that final darkness alone.

I wasn't in the asteroid belt now, but time and distance mean very little to the dead. I'd heard them, once, on Earth. It was hardly surprising that I could hear them here, in Earth orbit, on a forgotten space station that once, a very long time ago, must have counted a few Gypsies among its pioneer crew. And although I'd never before heard the song they were singing now, I knew what it meant. I'd pushed my luck too far, this time. I'd got burned too badly, too far from help. Michael couldn't drag me out of that tunnel by himself, and I hadn't the strength to drag myself.

Somehow I had never thought it would hurt so much.

"What would?" asked Michael.

I hadn't meant to speak aloud. It took a moment to realize I had, and that now I was expected to answer his question. "Oh," I said absently. "Just dying."

"You're not dying," he said.

"Sure." The living are so determined to cling to what they think they have. I smiled tolerantly to myself, in the darkness.

"Melacha."

"Oh, sorry." I had forgotten to give myself another push toward his distant goals. I put my hand against the wall and pushed, but there wasn't much strength in it, and I didn't really care anymore. It was more interesting to listen to the Gypsies sing.

Something bumped against my head, very gently. "Can you take hold of my foot?"

"Is that your foot?" I think I giggled. It seemed

very silly to be speaking of feet in the spangled darkness that had begun to encroach on my mind.

"Take hold of it, Melacha. You have one good hand. Use it."

I maneuvered my arm up over my head lazily, obediently, and draped my wrist across his ankle, and listened to the Gypsies.

"Good. Now hook your fingers over the top of my boot."

That was very complicated, but he insisted, and eventually I achieved what he wanted, so that he would quiet down and let me hear the music. "I'm cold," I said plaintively. "Let me go, Michael."

"Hold on, damn you." He moved forward again, dragging me with him. The edge of his flight boot cut into my fingers. I wanted to let go, but at his insistence I had wedged my fingers in hard against his leg, and even when I relaxed my hand it didn't come loose. "I still have a first aid kit," he said. "I can help you, when we get out of the tubes. But you have to hold on till then."

I think I answered him, but I haven't any idea what I said. I couldn't tell whether I was holding on, and it didn't really matter. I couldn't be bothered to exert any more energy, even to please him. If he spoke again, I didn't hear him; I heard only the Gypsies, and the distant rush of the winds of space, and the crystal whisper of stars I would never see again.

The darkness wasn't cold anymore; or, if it was, I didn't notice. The Gypsies sang me warm. They sang me companionship. They sang me the universe, and I reached out to take it, and I think I laughed out loud when my fingers closed on the light.

CHAPTER SEVENTEEN

I'd told him I never wanted to see a maintenance tube again. He must have believed me. He didn't just drag me into the first safe chamber out of the tubes and minister to my needs with the hatch left open to stare blackly into my face when I opened my eyes. He closed the hatch, and made sure the chamber we were in was not just secure, but well lighted and roomy enough that I wouldn't feel the smallest hint of claustrophobia. I hadn't said I suffered that, but I had said I was afraid of the dark.

He probably shouldn't have taken the time to soothe my fragile psyche before he tended to the much more crucial business of keeping my body alive, but a big part of staying alive does depend on a desire to stay alive. If I'd opened my eyes onto the stifling black narrowness of the maintenance tubes, I just might not have fought quite so hard to keep my eyes open and hang onto life. I think I would have; I'm hell of hardy, a survivor type from way back, and it takes more than a little weariness and a pretty death song and a lot of pain to make me give up for good; but he didn't know that.

The last time he'd seen me, I'd reeked of self-pity and survivor guilt; it was right after Django died. For all Michael knew, judging by that sample of my behavior, I didn't need much of an excuse at all to die. He got rid of all the excuses he could, before he gave me another dose of painkiller and a healthy jolt of the stuff known familiarly, in the Belt, as jockeyjuice.

It's a stimulant, among other things, and although it can help combat shock and keep a person functional in an emergency, it's absolutely not recommended for use with painkillers (a recommendation routinely ignored by everyone), and it doesn't last forever. It tends to wear off quite suddenly. One is encouraged to find a Sick Bay before that happens. One is encouraged to perform a lot of improbable tasks, by the med-techs who dream up these things and then seem surprised when we use them.

What I saw when I opened my eyes wasn't exactly a Belter's dream of heaven—there was too much metal and plastic, too little rock—but it was a far cry from the smothering tomb in which I'd passed out. There was plenty of room to move around in; he'd put me right in the center of a nice, big, airy chamber. And there was light. Blessed, cold, artificial blue light. And there was Michael, grinning anxiously at me, hovering and fretting. "How do you feel?" he asked solicitously.

"How the hell d'you think I feel?" I jackknifed just because I could, because there was room. "Where are we?"

He didn't comment on my lack of originality this

time. "We're in a rest area just off the flight deck. I secured the hatch. If there's any hue and cry outside, I didn't hear it. But I didn't take time to look over the flight deck. If they heard us, they'll be waiting."

"You mean if they heard us talk about stealing a shuttle? But even if they didn't, why didn't they just follow us right down the tubes?"

"They're Earthers."

"I know they're Earthers. And Earthers tend to be pretty damn dumb. But when they opened that chamber and didn't find us inside, and they knew we hadn't gone out through the control chamber, where the hell else would they look for us? The maintenance hatch was the only other way out."

"They may have figured that out, by now."

"Oh, come on, even Earthers aren't that dumb."

He looked patient, which meant he didn't feel patient. "Think about it from a dirt-dweller's standpoint. Think about all day gravity; full Earth gravity. Think about trying to maneuver through those tubes in that."

"Well, you couldn't, of course. But you don't have to. This is a freefall station, in case you hadn't noticed."

"People believe what they're accustomed to believing. To somebody accustomed to thinking in terms of gravity, those tubes are just plain impassable. At least, that's how they'd look. If somebody actually climbed in and started along them, he'd find out they're not, but it would take an innovative Earther to even try it."

"I suppose you're right. Anyway, they don't seem to have followed us. Which only means they'll be all the more surely waiting for us on the flight deck. Did you have a plan?" I was resisting the impulse to bounce off the walls like Collis. The combination of strong medication and freedom from the maintenance tubes left me with a heady sense of well-being.

"Just what you said before: we'll steal a shuttle and run like hell."

"Past the angry hordes without fear or hesitation? Well, I feel right now like we could do it, but I've used jockeyjuice before. The trick is to remember you're not really endowed with magical super-powers, you just think you are. Don't you think maybe we should refine the plan just a little bit?"

"What, and spoil the spontaneity?"

"I suppose there's always that."

He grinned suddenly. "Actually, now that you're safely out of the tubes, there is another possibility. It would mean leaving you here alone, though, and unarmed, since we are unarmed, and even though I've secured the hatch, they could get in if they wanted to."

"I thought you said Earthers wouldn't try the tubes."

He looked puzzled. "What does that have to do with anything?"

"Well, what's it matter if the hatch is secured?"

"*That* hatch." He pointed to the door.

"Oh. Sorry. I guess my Earther upbringing is showing."

He shook his head ruefully. "Only the Skyrider."

"What's that supposed to mean?"

"It's another affectation, isn't it? You only lived ten years on Earth. In twenty years in the Belt, I think you'd have picked up the local terminology if you wanted to. But you like to puzzle people, don't you?"

That was just a little too close for comfort. It's not so much that I like to puzzle people as it is that I like to keep them at a distance, but he had the general idea. He would. We'd been maintaining friendship by correspondence chips for a good many years now, and though our letters were infrequent, they were seldom just idle chatter. And he'd always been too damn perceptive for comfort. "Tell it to the psychtenders," I said crossly. "What's this plan that leaves me alone and unarmed behind an inefficiently secured *hatch* while you do . . . what? Go back into the tubes? What for?"

"To spy on the flight deck. And to see if I can promote us a weapon or two. We'll need something to get us from here to a shuttle, and safely on board." He was looking at me with an odd little challenging grin, but I wasn't sure whether the challenge applied to his proposed plan, or to the things he'd already said. I decided to ignore it.

"I assume you have some reason to believe you can do that without getting yourself killed?"

"I've lived in those tubes. I know every exit. If I can't catch one of those Earthers unaware, and disarm him, her, or it, I'm ready for retirement."

"I hate waiting," I said.

"You know I don't like that word."

It was a quirk he'd had since the war. He'd never said why, but he could not tolerate that word in silence. I hadn't forgotten. "What word? Hate? It's just a word, like war and death and love and rocks. If I removed from my vocabulary every word somebody didn't like, I'd end up with no words at all."

His look told me he knew I hadn't forgotten. "It might be an improvement, at that." He smiled faintly. "Whatsamatta you? Did I get too close?"

"Damn you." I said it without force or conviction. "I won't just float here and wait while you go off performing heroics. Think of another plan."

"You want some of the glory, is that it?"

He was really pushing for a fight, and I didn't see why. "I don't give a damn about glory. If you see any, keep it to yourself. What I want is some of the action."

"We could go charging out the door, hurling our worst Colonial curses, and see if that knocks the opposition out of the way. Belters are said to be good with curses, but of course you'd have to coach me."

"We could just sneak out."

"And get shot."

"If you can sneak out of a tube and disarm an Earther, why can't you sneak out of this chamber and disarm an Earther?"

"This chamber isn't quite as strategically located as some of the tube hatches are."

It wasn't the words, it was the way he looked at me that gave him away. "I see. And that's why you're trying to pick a fight. To get me angry enough to go back into the tubes." I shook my head. "It wasn't necessary, Michael. It wasn't necessary, and it won't work. If there really weren't another decent alternative, I'd tackle the damn tubes, but there is. There's plenty of alternatives. Look, even if the Earthers can't figure out how to travel the tubes themselves, by now they have to know we did. I mean, how the hell else did we get out of that chamber? So they may not come charging down the tubes after us, but they'll sure as space keep guard on strategically located hatches. They'll expect us to show up that way. They won't expect us to come casually down a rest area corridor."

"They'll expect us anywhere they see us." He

hadn't thought of that, and he was half convinced, but he didn't like it. His face said all that. It also said he hoped I could answer his objection.

"They'll expect two fugitives. What about two pilots?" I moved toward the closed cabinets on one wall of our chamber.

He looked at me in surprise. "You don't think you'll find flight suits, just our size, conveniently stored here, for space sake? I checked a few of the cabinets. They're empty."

I grinned. "It was a possibility, but no, I didn't expect it. Did you check all the cabinets?"

"No."

"Then let's do it. Maybe we can't expect flight suits, but there might be something."

There wasn't anything in any of the cabinets I checked. No flight suits, no weapons, nothing. Which was just what you'd expect on a deserted space station, but I was disappointed. "Well, it was worth a try," I said, closing the last door on my end of the row.

"It was better than that." He'd found a tool kit in one of the cabinets, and dragged it out into the light, looking smug.

"What in space can you do with that clutter?"

He opened the kit. It contained the standard complement of wrenches, nuts, bolts, and bits of plasteel wire, all of which started floating out into the chamber while we watched. "The straps on that leg brace are elastic, aren't they?"

"Well, some are," I said dubiously. "So what?"

"So I think we have a weapon. Maybe not much of one, but better than none. Take off the brace, will you?"

"Not without help." I couldn't reach all the fastenings, nor manage them one-handed if I could have reached them. "What kind of weapon are you going to make out of a bunch of old wrenches?"

"It's the bolts I want." He snapped the tool kit closed and floated across to me, to help unfasten the brace. "Save the straps. And this bit of plasteel, where the two verticals meet. Help me disconnect it. Hell, maybe we need the wrenches after all. I can't get this wing nut started. Hang onto it. There. No, I don't need the rest; just this bit, and the straps." He discarded most of the brace, retaining only a Y-shaped piece of plasteel and the strongest, stretchiest pieces of strap. "Now if I can just fasten these securely enough . . ."

"Oh, jeez," I said. "A *sling*shot? You're going to tackle the whole War Agency with an improvised slingshot?"

"You got any better ideas?" He was struggling with the straps, trying to tie them to the ends of the Y. "The hardware in that kit will make fine ammunition."

"I'm trapped on an antique space station with a Boy Scout."

"If you've got any better ideas, I'm listening."

"Well, for one thing, that's the wrong kind of knot." I showed him one that would work. "For another, how the hell are you going to brace yourself to aim the damn thing?" In freefall, a slingshot would be a very difficult weapon to use; one would need both hands to fire it, leaving none to cling to a handhold. A chance air current or an inadvertent twitch on the part of the user would throw the aim off completely.

"If I can make it, I can aim it," he said. "The question is, can you carry the ammunition?"

"Don't be silly, of course I can. I can even hand it to you, as wanted. D'you really think our targets are going to hang loose and let you shoot them? I mean, they're kind of likely to have a few slightly more advanced weapons than this, aren't they?"

"Don't let your fondness for modern technology blind you to the advantages of the primitive. A good man with a slingshot can be something to reckon with."

"Sure. David and Goliath and that. I'd still rather have a laser."

"I'd settle for a stun gun. Here, hold this." He thrust the tool kit into my arms. "Now here's the plan. We're about three doors down from the flight deck. There's a ready-room across the corridor from us. I didn't take you there because I didn't know how many folks we might meet inside. But we'd have a better chance on the flight deck if we could change our costumes before we head for a shuttle. It would be a particularly good idea to hide all this damn burn plaster. So we'll try the ready-room, and see if we can't promote a couple of flight suits. Failing that, we'll go straight for the flight deck and grab the first shuttle on line. I'm assuming you can fly just about anything they've got?"

"I can fly *any*thing they've got."

He grinned. "Even one-handed, hotshot?"

"You damn betcha."

"Okay. If it's something standard, a Starbird or a Falcon, I can fly it, but I don't have any experience with those damn Fords you fly in the Belt."

"They're easy. Only they do tend to wallow. Michael?"

"Yeah?"

"If they've got a Sunfinch, I'm going for it."

He studied my expression. "You'll get us killed yet."

"Maybe. But I'm going for it, if it's there. And if I do, I think you should go ahead with the first one you see that you can fly. If we get out of here at all, we may just need two birds. We certainly will, if one of them's a Sunfinch. I'll need you to cover for me, in that case."

He shook his head. "They won't have a Sunfinch, anyway. Only Earther officials—very official Earther officials—have Sunfinches."

I grinned. "You're forgetting this is an Earther agency we're dealing with. What's more, if they do have a Sunfinch, and I can get away with it, they'll have a hard time claiming it back, won't they? Unless they're ready to admit they're Earthers."

He looked tough and determined and a little puzzled. "Well, you can hope, I guess. I'll be happy if we just get out of here alive. You ready?"

"I'm ready."

He opened the door.

CHAPTER EIGHTEEN

We went out fast and low, which only proved that we were both accustomed to conducting our battles in gravity situations. "Low" with relation to our previous positions turned out to be "high" with relation to the people in the corridor. It worked, though. Michael hit two of them with his improvised slingshot before they figured out where we were; they were a lot less accustomed to freefall than we were.

By the time they figured out where we were, they also figured out they were getting hit; and that confused them, I think, because they couldn't see what we were hitting them with. I doubt they saw any connection between the absurd contraption in Michael's hands and the fact that two of their number were suddenly bleeding. Projectile weapons are uncommon to start with, and they look just like ordinary handguns, which neither Michael nor I was holding. Yet one of our adversaries had a broken nose and was rapidly choking to death on her own blood, another had both hands up to cover a badly damaged eye; and while they tried to figure it out, Michael hit a third one solidly on the neck.

There were six of them altogether, and the three who hadn't been hit were scared. Our weapon was a good deal less effective than theirs, but they didn't understand it. They panicked. Their shots went wild, and we got across the corridor alive.

The ready-room door was open. I plunged right on through while Michael took up a position in the doorway, partially shielded from the corridor, and lobbed a few more nuts and bolts at the confused agents we'd come past. There were half a dozen more of the same in the ready-room, scattered around in various stages of undress. My initial plunge into the chamber carried me straight across to a woman half in, half out of a flight suit.

She never had a chance. She had her weapon off, and although she thought quickly and moved quickly, I was just a little quicker. That's all it took. She had the weapon in her hand when I hit her. She hadn't got it aimed yet. She never did. I collided with her and grabbed the weapon, hooked my bad leg across both of hers and my good one on the door of her locker for leverage, and bent her arm back till the laser in her hand was aimed at her head. She did the rest for me. It happened so fast, she must never have realized where the thing was pointed. She just pulled the firing button and died.

I didn't stop to think about it. There were five others in that chamber with me, and I figured they were all armed. Before the first one had finished dying, I had the laser out of her hand and had fired at the next three nearest me. I got the first two. The third one ducked behind a row of lockers so my shot at him didn't singe anything but paint. By then, he and the other two live ones had all had a chance to fire at me, but they hadn't been practicing on moving targets. One of them knocked some of the burn plaster off my bad leg, but I didn't notice that till later. The others didn't even come close.

Off to my right somewhere, Michael dived in from the doorway, and one of the hidden Earthers exposed herself to get a shot at him. I steadied myself against a locker and blasted her. That left two live ones, plus whoever might come through the door after Michael. He said something to me, but I didn't catch the words. The Earthers were retreating nervously before us. Michael got a clear shot at one, and took it. That left one.

"Don't shoot!" he said. His voice was thin and reedy with fright. I sighted toward the sound of it. "I've lost my laser. Don't shoot. I'm unarmed."

"Come out, then," said Michael.

I kept my laser balanced across a locker, aimed toward the Earther's voice. There was no sound behind me. I wanted to turn, to see if anyone had followed Michael into the chamber, but I didn't. First things first. The man who said he'd lost his laser didn't come straight out of hiding when Michael told him to. Why not? He might just have been scared, but I didn't believe it. Earthers do scare easy, but they're also the trickiest bastards in the Solar System.

"I'm unarmed," he said again. "Don't shoot."

I corrected my aim: he had moved sideways behind the lockers.

"Come out where we can see you," said Michael.

Maybe the Earther was hoping we would both speak, so he could tell where we were before he came blasting out of hiding. If so, he didn't get his

wish. And after one more appeal, to which Michael's
response was clearly impatient, he gave up on it.
Maybe he thought he could take Michael and still
have time to look around for me. Or maybe he meant
to keep his weapon hidden while he came out far
enough to spot us, then lift it and kill us both before
we could react. Either way, it was a faint chance at
best, and he didn't get to try it. When his head was
clear of the lockers, I shot him and turned to face the
door.

"He was surrendering!" Michael's voice was harsh
with surprise.

"Sure he was. What did you do with the ones in
the corridor?"

"He was unarmed." He was staring from me to
the dead man and back again like he'd never seen
anyone killed before: he, who had just killed several.
"He was giving up and you shot him." This was the
civilized Michael again, tricked into existence by the
ritual phrases of surrender.

"Don't be a fool. He was armed. What happened
to the ones outside?"

He didn't want to talk about the ones outside.
"Damn it, he surrendered." It wasn't an entirely
boyish face that stared at me; there was a warrior's
anger in his eyes. But Colonial Warriors fight "fair."

"Oh, for space sake, Michael, take a look at the
man. I'll bet his laser's still clutched in his greasy
Earther fingers. I don't like killing, but by God I
know when it has to be done. They don't surrender
that easy, and you know it."

Michael kicked away from the lockers next to him,
to go to the dead Earther. There was a silence while
he found the laser, thought about it, and turned back
to me. "You couldn't have known he was still armed."

"If he hadn't been, he'd have taken the first opportunity to arm himself. We're hardly equipped to take prisoners, and I don't happen to have a stun gun. He was the enemy and I shot him. Since when is that a crime?"

"Since he offered to surrender."

"I don't believe we're having this conversation. What the hell do you want? What difference does it make what a man's talking about, or what he's doing with his hands, or which way he's facing, when you kill him? He had to be killed. Dead is dead. If I waited for every bad guy to face my direction and show me his weapon before I killed him, I'd be dead by now. You been reading some damn rule book, or something? Don't you know there *aren't* any rules, except staying alive? Jeez. If you stop to cry about every damn dead enemy, no wonder you lost the war." All right, so the lady maybe protested a little too much. I've said I don't like killing.

"This isn't war," he said.

"What is it, then? It sure as space isn't peace."

He looked toward the corridor. "There's nobody out there right now, but there probably will be soon, because I didn't even hit all of them, much less kill them." He said that with an odd, sideways glance at me, fraught with meaning that I didn't understand. "We'd better grab some weapons and a couple of flight suits and get the hell out of here in a hurry."

I didn't ask whether that meant I was forgiven for killing the Earther. I was too vexed with Michael to care. I found a flight suit in one of the lockers and struggled to get in it; it was too big for me, but that was as well, since it meant it would go on easily over the burn plaster and my tunic, which I hadn't bothered to remove. The fastenings were velcro, which was lucky; I couldn't have managed buttons or a zipper with only one hand. As it was, I had to let go of my commandeered laser to dress. It kept floating away, and I kept trying to follow, not wanting to be far from it when somebody came charging in through the door to blast us out of there.

Michael, having two hands, dressed faster than I did, and went around the chamber collecting the rest of the weapons that were floating loose while I was still playing hide-and-seek with the one I had. When I was dressed he gave me two more lasers and kept three for himself. Nobody came near the door the whole time.

"Now that they know we're out of the tubes, we could go back in them," he said. "There's a hatch here, and it's straight from here to the flight deck."

"No way. They won't stop guarding the hatches just because we've shown ourselves here."

He shrugged. "You got a better idea?"

"Yeah. We go straight down the corridor, take out anybody who gets in our way, grab the first shuttle we see—unless there's a Sunfinch, in which case we grab two—and get the hell off this station."

"Sounds easy enough." He was studying me expressionlessly.

I grinned. "Does, doesn't it? Too bad it won't be."

"I wondered whether you'd thought of that."

"Space, yes. But I'm not going back into those tubes."

He hesitated. "You were right. About the Earther."

"I know that." I grinned. "Being polite won't get me back in the tubes, either."

"Well, hell," he said, and smiled. Not the boy's

smile, but the wolf's. "I never expected to live forever, anyway, I guess. You ready?"

I felt ready for just about anything, but I didn't have to be. There was nobody in the corridor when we went out. We looked at each other and headed for the flight deck, closing the ready-room door behind us to delay discovery of the carnage we left in our wake. The jockeyjuice was still keeping me alert and energetic, but I could tell, now, that it would soon begin to fray at the edges; and I wondered whether we could get onto a liberated shuttle before the jockeyjuice deserted me completely and I crumpled into a useless, worn-out lump of burned flesh and aching bones.

We made it all the way to the flight deck before we ran into any opposition. And there was a Sunfinch on the panels, just waiting for me to take it. I pointed it out to Michael before we both had to duck for cover from the laser blasts of the Earthers who spotted us. "That's mine," I said.

If everything had gone according to the original plan, and Michael and I had left the station on the *Defiance* with Jamin and the hostages, I would have held the hostages hostage to see if I could get the Company to give me a Sunfinch. Hell, it might even have worked; I tried to keep everyone guessing as to just how soft- or hard-hearted I really was, and those were high muckymuck hostages. Earth might not have let the C.I.D. blast me. The high muckymucks whose hostages I would have held would certainly have had something to say about it.

However, at this point I'd lost the damn hostages, and the only real hope I saw of getting a Sunfinch was to steal one from the War Agency. If they hadn't had one to steal, I'd have thought of something else, I suppose; I'd told Michael I would get one. Luckily, I didn't have to look any farther. They did have one.

"That's halfway across the deck," said Michael. "You can't get to it. There's a Starbird nearer, lined up for breakaway. Let's take that."

"You take that," I said. We were both firing more or less at random onto the flight deck; the Earthers were not yet ready to expose themselves in order to fire on us. Probably they were waiting for reinforcements to take us from the rear. "I'm taking the Sunfinch. You said we needed it."

He was keeping an eye on the corridor behind us, and snapped off a shot at some movement he saw there in the distance. "Don't be a goddamn hero," he said. "We need it, all right, but you can't get it, so why the hell die trying?"

"I can get it," I said.

He shot again at the end of the corridor, turned to fire onto the flight deck, and paused to look at me. "Jockeyjuice," he said.

I shrugged. "Maybe. Get that Starbird and cover for me, and we'll see."

"Goddamn," he said.

"That, too," I said. "If I make it, you cover me good, because both fleets outside may go for me at first."

He didn't look at me again. "If you make it, you just run like hell for Mars; I'll handle the fleets."

"Both of them? All by yourself? Now who's the hero?"

"Oh, hell," he said. "Just do it."

"Sure. You ready?"

"I'm ready." He looked ready. He had a laser in each hand and a daredevil grin on his face. There was, after all, a hint of the boy's wild excitement in the warrior's pale eyes.

''Let's go, then.'' We hit the flight deck with all three lasers burning us a path.

CHAPTER NINETEEN

The War Agency put up a respectable struggle for that Sunfinch. She was a pretty shuttle, sleeker and more elegant than I'd realized from the brief glimpses I'd had of them in space. In the Belt, most of the working shuttles were ugly, boxy affairs, designed for maximum load capacity and fuel efficiency. The most atmosphere they ever had to buck was that on a flight deck, so there was no reason for streamlining aerodynamics. But the Sunfinch was built to take anything.

The basic construction was solid; a rugged box that could carry a rough load a long distance. The box was pulled out of shape the long way, into smooth long lines that would pierce a planet's atmosphere like an arrow; with great broad wings folded back against the sides on the flight deck that would extend from the sides and lock into place to catch and conquer the fierce buffeting winds of any habitable planet. The nose was drawn out to a blunt needle point forward of the cockpit, and the tail bulged with nacelles housing powerful engines that could pull the ship out of a gravity well or outfly even a Falcon like the *Defiance* in open space.

My desire to steal that beauty wasn't based entirely on military necessity. I wanted to fly her. I wanted to feel the swift obedience of her controls under my hands. I wanted to spread those wings and plummet down through an atmosphere, just to experience the tug and pull of her jockeystick and the wild, mad song of the challenged winds. Even if the Colonials hadn't needed a Sunfinch to win the war, I'd have taken that demure beauty off that flight deck if I could.

The I.D. numbers painted across her streamlined tail said she was the same swift Sunfinch that had passed us on our way to Station Newhome, and I wondered briefly what embarrassed Earther mucky-mucks would be trapped out here with slower transportation back, when I'd snatched her out from under their noses. It didn't really matter. They would find an explanation for their absence from Earth, and nobody would question them very much about it, and I didn't give a damn if somebody did.

Michael wished me luck when he turned toward the Starbird he'd selected. I barely noticed, beyond absently wishing him luck in return. I was watching the Sunfinch and her protectors. They were numerous, and not because she was beautiful. If they weren't pilots, they might not even recognize her beauty. To Earth, she was an advancement in technology that the Colonies must not be allowed to obtain.

There were half a dozen women in Martian dress strung out along her far side, shooting at me from under her plump belly. Beyond them, another half dozen in Belter dress, mostly men, were angling for position, but none of them had a clear shot at me. Off to one side, concealed behind a battered old Belter Chevy, were some people in what looked like Earther flight suits, some of them shooting and some of them apparently just observing. And overhead, in the cavernous regions above the parked shuttles, Earthers in various costumes floated among the structural supports and tried to hide in the shadows, some of them maybe going after Michael, but most of them trying to keep me from the Sunfinch.

They were a poorly trained army. They could all have benefited from a few hours on a target range; and most of them had the awkward bravado of people who have never before engaged in a firefight with live weapons. If you survive that first fight, you're a warrior. But it is a dividing line. If you've never shot a human target before, you can't tell how you'll react when the time comes.

Over the years I'd survived a few firefights, but it wasn't primarily superior fighting ability that saved me this time; it was more like superior indifference. I really didn't give a damn, at the time, what happened to me: I meant to have that Sunfinch or die trying. If I'd thought it out that clearly, in words, I'd have changed my mind; but I didn't. I just wanted that Sunfinch, and went for it.

Some people insist that indifference is the real separation between seasoned warriors and amateurs. Maybe it is. I killed more than one agent that day just because I was willing to expose myself to get the shot. It helped that I had a better aim than most of them. But really, I don't know what got me across that deck alive.

For the most part, the fighting was too quick and confused to single out separate incidents for retelling. I kept firing the laser I held till the gauge turned red, threw it away, and drew my second one. When I could, I took cover behind parked shuttles; and when I had to, I floated fast through the clear spaces between them; and every move brought me nearer that beautiful sleek Sunfinch.

When my second laser's gauge turned red, I was close enough to one of the Earthers to throw it at her. The air around me stank of burnt plastic and people. My eyes were dazzled by the constant laser fire, and my nose and eyes ached from dryness and the sharp tang of sealant somebody had got out to cover a hole somebody else had burned in the bulkhead off somewhere to my right. My mouth was dry, and tasted of gritty smoke and sweat and anger. With my good hand constantly occupied with a laser, I had to use the burned one for balance, catching at handholds, and pushing off to float when I couldn't find anything to kick against. It had begun to ache dully, and the arm felt heavy and numb to the shoulder.

Then I was at the Sunfinch's forward hatch, fumbling with the locking mechanism with my burned hand, and still blasting Earthers with the laser in the other. My ears popped, and I knew that either Michael had escaped in his Starbird or someone else had popped the landing deck's force field, coming or going, and I tasted the hot oil and malite of working engines, and the Sunfinch's hatch came open under my hands.

Somebody shouted. I fired automatically at the sound, not even looking to see if the blast connected. Somebody fired close enough to singe the sleeve of my flight suit before I pulled myself inside and closed the hatch behind me. There wasn't time to program the computer to lock securely against broaders, so I fired the engines with the laser in my hand. When an Earther came floating into the cockpit from the passenger compartment I turned the barrel toward her without even thinking.

She said, "Don't do it," and something in her tone kept me from pulling the firing button. I looked at her. She held up her hands, showing me she was unarmed, and took the navigator's seat beside me. "You can space me later if you decide you have to," she said, fastening her shock webbing and smiling an odd, sideways smile at me.

"What the hell?" I said.

"You ever flown a Sunfinch before?" she asked. She was a tall, rangy woman with a horsy sort of face and eyes lined all around from smiling that cheerful, carefree, friendly smile. Her hair was about an inch long and frizzy, forming a stiff black halo like static electricity, which made her face look longer and horsier and her smile whiter and crazier. And she was wearing a complete Earth Fighter Captain's uniform, with campaign ribbons over the pocket and a marksmanship crossed-beam pin on the collar.

"Are you offering lessons?" I asked.

"Better let the pressure off the converter," she said. "Gauge by your left knee. Don't let it ride past fifteen hundred or we'll blow a gasket."

Somebody opened the hatch beside her. She reacted as if we'd rehearsed it. I turned to fire, she leaned forward to give me a clear shot, I turned back to the instruments, and she kicked the body out the hatch and pulled the cover shut again.

"Good shot," she said. "Watch the laser gauges. They're hooked directly into the converter. Name's

Jake, pleased to meet you. Thing here controls the panel snags, same like on a Falcon. Oh, and you got two auxilliary screens over here.'' She snapped them on, showing us a view of converging War Agency personnel on either side of the shuttle. "Looks like we'd better get out of here and leave the orientation lecture for later."

If I'd had time, I'd have liked to kick her and her orientation lecture right out of the cockpit. I didn't have any idea why I hadn't killed her; it would only be more trouble later. When I glanced at her while I was releasing the panel snags, she was grinning at me again. She knew what I was thinking, and it didn't bother her a bit.

By the time I'd wrestled the Sunfinch off the panel, I thought I was pretty well acquainted with all the quirks of her controls, and I knew I was in love. Even my sweet *Defiance* couldn't compete with a Sunfinch. Jake settled in comfortably against her shock straps and grinned at me again. "Flies loose, doesn't she?"

"You damn betcha," I said absently. Now that we were off the panels, the computer had locked the hatches for flight and I didn't have to worry about boarders anymore. I put the last laser in my belt and watched the screens.

The War Agency's poorly trained personnel didn't seem to know quite what to do. They clustered around the Sunfinch, firing on us with handguns, which was so much wasted energy; the exterior that was designed to withstand the rigors of an atmospheric entry couldn't be marked by hand lasers.

A few of them figured it out, and went for the other shuttles up and down the panels, but they couldn't fire on us from them till we'd popped the force screen. Using the big guns inside the station could blow it apart. Since I didn't give a damn about Station Newhome, I could have floated right there and blasted them all off the panels, but I didn't. Quite aside from any other consideration, there was the possibility that if Newhome took too bad a hit and really did start coming apart at the seams, it just might take us with it.

The alternative was to pop the screen and see what happened once we were outside. The flight deck was, to all appearances, an open-sided tunnel from space into Unit Six, but in fact the open side was covered with an invisible force screen that reacted automatically with alloys in a shuttle's hull, letting the shuttles pass in and out but retaining the atmosphere inside the station. From where we floated, inside, I couldn't see the fleets that were gathered outside, and I wasn't sure what to expect from them.

I let the War Agency's shuttles find out for me. A couple of Starbirds, clumsily painted with the blazon of the Colonial Fleet, and a battered old Datsun that hadn't seen any kind of paint in a very long time, all decided to pop the screen and wait for me outside. I watched them go, and waited to see what the fleets out there would do about it.

They didn't do anything. Well, that was promising. If they would do exactly the same for me, we'd be home free. All I'd have to fight would be the War Agency shuttles, and if the fleets didn't interfere, I'd just outrun them all.

After waiting a long moment to be sure nobody was going to attack the shuttles ahead of me, I moved up on the screen and popped it gently, staying as close to the station as I could to keep the War Agency shuttles outside from firing. Those still inside could take pot shots at me if they dared. I didn't think they would; aiming a laser or even a photar through an atmosphere shield can be a chancy business, pretty sophisticated for fighters as inexperienced as most of these were.

The two fleets, Earth Fighters on one side and Colonial Warriors on the other, glittered against the backdrop of stars: hundreds of shuttles in all colors and sizes and makes, all lined up on either side of the station, bristling with weapons, trying to stare each other down. I tried the Comm Link on both Colonial and Company frequencies, just listening. Nobody said a word.

"Aren't you gonna identify yourself?" asked Jake.

I glanced at her. "I wish I had time to ask that of you." A War Agency Starbird popped the screen to one side of us, found its field of fire reasonably clear, and fired its photars at me. I jumped aside easily, delighting in the Sunfinch's quick obedience and grace.

When I had time to look at the screens again, I was less delighted. The two fleets floated serenely against the stars, apparently indifferent to me, the station behind me, and the various shuttles angling for position to fire on me. But they weren't indifferent. They were dead silent, and they weren't firing on me or on each other, but they had moved while I wasn't looking. Together they now formed a neat, complete, patient, and perfect hollow sphere, with me and the War Agency inside it and no visible way out, even for a Sunfinch.

Within the sphere, War Agency shuttles were patiently lining up for the kill; and I was their only target.

CHAPTER TWENTY

I had plenty of room inside the sphere to maneuver; and with the War Agency shuttles coming after me from several directions at once, I needed it. I thought that if I could get out from under their guns for long enough, I could punch a hole through the sphere and fight my way out, though I wasn't sure how either fleet would react if I tried. It wasn't an immediate problem; first I had to deal with the War Agency.

One of their shuttles fired on me from behind. I flipped the Sunfinch over, dodging the blast and riding backward long enough to return fire, trying out my new guns. They worked fine. Scratch one War Agency shuttle. I scanned the rest of them, trying to find the Starbird Michael had taken. There wasn't time for a thorough study; there was a Ford angling for a firing position on one side of me, and a Falcon taking potshots from the other.

The Sunfinch responded with delicate precision to

my clumsy, one-handed guidance. She was graceful in spite of her bulk, and her incredible power was a delight. The combination of control and potential was exhilarating. The Falcon's potshots didn't even singe her paint.

We slid sideways across the open center of the sphere till I could get an angle on the Falcon that didn't endanger any other ships. The Ford followed us awkwardly, ancient and slow. At the last minute, the pilot of the Falcon saw what I was doing; but it was too late. Scratch another Agency shuttle.

The Ford's pilot had her in hand now, closing on me. I flipped the Sunfinch again, letting her ride back across the sphere, keeping the Ford off balance, watching for Michael.

He came out of the space beside Station Newhome in a quick dive that took him past the Ford in firing range; and he got her, the blast carefully calculated so that none of the ships in either fleet were damaged. Another Agency Starbird followed him out, hanging fire till the angle was right.

I jockeyed forward, but I couldn't get an angle on the enemy Starbird that didn't endanger Michael. A Colonial Warrior slid cautiously out of place in the sphere, angling for position on the Starbird that was tracking Michael. An Earth Fighter Starbird immediately jockeyed in toward the Colonial; obviously, the Earthers didn't want anybody interfering with our miniature battle.

I got the angle, and took out the Starbird before it caught Michael. Beside me, Jake said, "Watch it. Earthers up to something."

I didn't look at her. "Aren't you an Earther?" But I didn't listen to her answer, if any: the Earthers were indeed up to something. Half a dozen of them were easing out of their places in the sphere, while the others closed ranks behind them. A War Agency shuttle took my attention from them for a moment. When I looked back, the six Earthers who had separated from their fleet were approaching us in attack formation.

"Colonials can't interfere, but you can?" I said it aloud, but the Comm Link didn't respond. The Earthers dived, and I didn't have time after that to worry about the rules of the game. I was busy staying alive.

They made no effort to separate Michael and me from the other Agency shuttles, nor to direct their fire in such a way as to limit damage to the Colonial half of the sphere that surrounded us. One sleek Falcon got on my tail and it took all the Sunfinch's phenomenal maneuverability to dodge it in the confines of the sphere. I couldn't get an angle to fire; all I could do was stay out of the Falcon's angle.

It was time to introduce ourselves, though by now I was confident the Colonials, at least, had figured out which of us were whom. Maybe the Earthers had, too, and didn't like to admit it. Anyway, so nobody could pretend further ignorance, Michael and I both identified ourselves and our shuttles while we dodged Earther and Agency ships alike. The Earthers weren't slowed by the information, but the Colonials finally took action. They were apparently on the EF Comm Link frequency, and I heard one of them say crossly, "Why in space didn't you say so before? We couldn't move till we were sure, you know."

I made a sound someone might have mistaken for laughter. "I've been busy." Michael didn't say anything; he was still busy. An EF tried to take him out, and he had to flip and slide backward half across the sphere before he got a safe angle to fire delicately across her nose, warning her without harming anyone.

"What in space is going on here?" I dodged an EF of my own. "Hey, guys. Remember me? I'm the Skyrider, the one who just rescued your hostages. And that's my cousin Michael, without whom I wouldn't be here to play games with you. I understand it's Earth's policy to shoot down just about anybody, on whim, but what the hell are you Colonials doing? Are you going to leave Michael and me to fight off terrorists and EFs both, all by ourselves? Would it make any difference if I reminded you that some of those hostages were Colonials?"

The Colonials didn't take long to think about it. I was fighting off another Agency shuttle when they made their first move, but when I could look around again, there were six Colonials to match the six EFs who'd left their places in the sphere. The Colonials chased the EFs back from the battle, but that was all they could do; the EFs wouldn't let them help us against the Agency shuttles that were still determined to stop us before I could get away with that Sunfinch.

Nobody seemed to care quite as much whether Michael got away in his Starbird, at least at first; but he made quite a nuisance of himself with it. For infighting like that, a Starbird was probably a better ship even than the Sunfinch, and Michael was a hell of a good pilot. They quit ignoring him right quickly.

But they couldn't catch him. And they couldn't catch me. Actually, once the Colonials got the EFs off our backs, I was having fun; that Sunfinch was quite a shuttle. She could flip end over end in half the space it took my Falcon, and with the extra power of the new malite converters we didn't have to ride backward if we didn't want to; a touch of a jockey thruster would overcome inertia like it didn't exist.

Her weapons were better focused than my Falcon's, too. It wasn't half the trouble I thought it would be to calculate angles and direct my fire so it hit Agency shuttles without danger of blasting right past them into the retaining sphere around us. I didn't want to hit any Colonials, and it wouldn't have been quite politic to take out any EFs just then even if I did want to; but in the Sunfinch, it wasn't a problem.

What was a problem was that the painkillers and jockeyjuice Michael had given me were wearing off, and even in a Sunfinch I wasn't keeping up anymore. Besides, the Agency shuttles Michael and I hadn't got in the first few minutes of battle were hell of good at what they did, and they'd had at least mock battles with the Sunfinch before. They knew full well what she could do, and how to counter her capabilities. They probably knew her better than I did. I didn't think they could kill me; but neither could I kill them. Stalemate. Unless I could get out of that damned sphere.

Michael cursed the fleets. The whole lot of them, on both sides of the sphere. He repeated who we were, why we were there, who the so-called terrorists were, and what they had done. Neither of us called the terrorists Earthers then, but Michael called them a lot of worse names, most of them unprintable; and he spread his comments liberally over the two fleets that refused to help us fight them or to let us escape them.

I'm afraid I laughed. I mean, it was funny, after all: the two great fleets squared off like that, but unwilling to battle each other; with the lot of us dancing our deadly little game of tag between them. If the EFs tried to interfere, Colonials stopped them;

and if Colonials tried, Earthers stopped them; all without a shot fired or a word exchanged. Just showy little battle dances, as though all our ships were great birds of prey engaged in rather sinister mating rituals. I laughed. And I told them what I thought of them. Jake stared at me as though she thought I'd gone crazy, but I didn't care. Maybe I had. Or maybe the rest of the world had.

Michael sidled his little Starbird up beside my Sunfinch, and we kept our noses to the Agency shuttles while they tried to get decent angles on us to fire. Between us, we were able to bunch them into a little group in front of the station. We stayed between them and the major area of the sphere, and when any of them tried to break away, we fired. We couldn't hit them, but we could scare them, and at that angle we didn't have to worry about hitting either of the fleets that imprisoned us. Michael stopped cursing; it wasn't doing anyone any good.

"Fine armies," I said. "You guys look real fierce out there, all formed up for a parade. These terrorists don't have any hostages anymore, so why should you interfere with anything they do? I mean, what's in it for you? Everybody knows Colonials and Earthers don't fight side by side; you're enemies. What would people think? Colonials and EFs collaborating? Why, hell, you might lose your Space Cadet badges over something like that.'' One of the Agency shuttles slipped sideways quite suddenly, and had an angle on Michael before either of us saw what was happening. I couldn't take him out without risking a Colonial shuttle beyond him, and when I reached for the jockey thrusters my hand was so unsteady I almost overjumped the angle I wanted. The Sunfinch skittered a little, but we scared the Agency shuttle back where it belonged.

"You cut that one close enough," said Michael.

"The jockeyjuice is wearing off," I said. When I'd made my move, I'd seen a Colonial start forward from the sphere; if I hadn't stopped the Agency shuttle, he might have. But he was neatly back in place now, his firepower once more trained on his opposite number on the EF side of the sphere. "The painkiller wore off a while ago. If these rock-happy soldiers don't stop playing dress-up and do something pretty damn soon, we've had it."

Jake glanced at me, but she didn't say anything. A stranger's voice cleared its throat over the Comm Link, but I hadn't time to attend to it; another Agency shuttle was trying to break loose. Again, when I went for it, I noticed a Colonial shuttle edging forward as if to back me up, and I thought I was going to need it this time; the Agency shuttle was after me, and I wasn't moving as fast as I should have been. The searing sparkle of a near-miss photar surrounded my Sunfinch before I knew anybody was firing.

"Spin out," said Michael. He was coming up on my side, but I was between him and the Agency shuttle. I reached for the controls to spin out of his way, but I couldn't even see them.

"Okay, Space Cadets," I said. "It's show time. Either you get in here and knock these terrorists out of my way, or I'll damn well ram them down your variegated throats. In case you hadn't noticed, the war hasn't started yet." I managed to spin the Sunfinch sideways, and she slid heavily like a grounded rock, just in time to dodge another photar blast. "But I'll start it here in a minute, just for excitement, if nobody else can think of anything to do."

"That's a Sunfinch you're flying," said a new voice, possibly the one that had cleared its throat.

I laughed again. "You ain't *seen* flying, yet. You'll know it when you see it. There'll be EFs from here to hell and gone, and you won't see me waiting around to pick up the pieces." The funny thing was, sick and sore and weary as I felt, I was enjoying myself. This was the sort of thing I lived for. Doubtless the sort of thing I'd die for one day, too; but that was half the fun. And if the fleets wouldn't help me against the Agency shuttles, I really was ready to start ramming them down somebody's throat.

"Where'd you get a Sunfinch?" asked another voice.

"I think the question here is, how long can I keep it?" I said as Michael fended another photar for me. "That is, how long can I keep it if I stay polite? I've been trying not to hurt anyone but terrorists, but I can't keep that up forever. Are you guys ready to play on my side, or d'you want to see how well you do against me? You'll have the terrorists to help you, of course, but that won't make it easy when I start really having fun." I didn't wait to see if any of them answered me. I wasn't sure I could wait. I couldn't see straight, I couldn't hear right, my one working arm wouldn't necessarily do what I wanted it to, and I could hear Gypsies singing all around that Sunfinch like they never sang except for danger or for death. It was a little late to be warning me of danger, so I figured they were singing about the other, and I was damned if I'd go out sitting still and waiting for the final photar or laser to send me to hell. I intended to take a few folks with me.

I dived for the bunched terrorists, and they scattered like wild rocks in a comet's path. I heard

Michael say something, but I didn't know what it was, and I wasn't about to stop and listen. I think I said something, too, but I might have been talking to the Gypsies.

The Agency shuttles panicked. I must really have looked crazy, then. There was no telling what I might do. Even I didn't know for sure. I blasted an old Ford on my first dive, and I singed more than one of the others. They didn't take time to return fire; they just ducked nervously out of my way.

When I was almost on the station, I flipped and hit the thrusters, playing with the space I had, feeling a bit hemmed in by the opposing fleets, but past the point of asking for help. I think I overshot my mark; Jake made a sound beside me, and I thought I saw Earthers slide out of my path to keep from getting hit, but I wasn't sure of it.

Somebody said, "She can't take them all by herself."

Somebody else laughed a little. "The Skyrider can." Maybe that was me; it was something I would say. But I wasn't paying attention to talk anymore. Not even my own. I aimed a laser at an Agency shuttle and had to cut the blast short to keep from hitting an EF Starbird beyond it. "If you won't fight, you could at least get out of the way," I said peevishly, forgetting I'd threatened to burn them all, and went right after another Agency shuttle that caught my wandering attention.

The Earther I hadn't shot was the first one to join the battle, but he wasn't far ahead of the others. Both fleets broke formation at once, and came after the Agency shuttles like somebody had given them a signal. Maybe somebody had. There were half a dozen more Agency shuttles coming out of Station

Newhome, and even I wasn't fool enough to think I could hold off that many by myself, or with only Michael's help. But the two fleets, fighting side by side, mopped up the area in no time.

I never was sure exactly what happened. When the fleets broke formation, the Gypsies stopped singing, so I figured I wasn't dead yet. I hadn't been sure; I wasn't feeling real lively. I settled back to watch the battle, but everything was muddled and blurred, and I really just have a couple of vivid memories of isolated incidents: an Agency shuttle closing on a Colonial, and an EF blasting him off the Colonial's tail; an EF, crippled, guided safely onto Newhome by a Colonial Starbird; and Michael, hovering protectively near me, saying something over the Comm Link that I couldn't quite understand.

Then there weren't any more Agency shuttles, and the Colonial and EF fleets were so intermingled they looked like one vast army. That was a magnificent alliance, and I floated there admiring the sight of them for several moments before I realized I'd missed my opportunity to take the Sunfinch and run.

I wasn't quite sure I could have if I'd tried, but I should have tried. In the confusion I might have been able to ram my way past both fleets and flee before anyone knew I was gone. If I went now that the battle was over, I'd have half the EF fleet on my tail before I knew it; and there were two or three Sunfinches among them, so I couldn't outrun them. Not in the condition I was in. I might still have tried it, had I been healthy, but I wasn't.

"Time to go home," somebody said.

"I don't think so," I said. My voice sounded thin and frail. I cleared my throat. I hadn't the smallest idea what I was going to do. But I wasn't giving up that Sunfinch without a fight.

Somebody read my mind. "Skyrider, that Sunfinch is official government property."

Beside me, Jake stirred, catching my attention for the first time since the sphere broke formation. She had on quite a fine EF uniform, complete with a great many medals and badges of rank.

Looking at her, I figured it out, and grinned. "Says who?"

CHAPTER TWENTY-ONE

I flipped off the Comm Link and grinned confi-
dently—at least, I hoped I looked confident—at Jake.
She looked startled, then puzzled, then faintly alarmed,
in rapid succession. "Come on, Skyrider, there's
limits to what even you can get away with."

"Maybe. Maybe not. If this Sunfinch is government property, how did the terrorists get it?"

"They aren't terrorists, they're an Earther agency,
and you know it."

That tended to clear up any residual doubts I'd had
about Jake. She looked like a loyal EF officer; but
she hadn't acted like one when she helped me steal
the Sunfinch off Newhome's flight deck; and she
didn't talk like one now. "I don't think the Company
would like to hear you talk like that," I said mildly.

"Space the government." She hesitated, frowning
at me in sudden comprehension. "Oh. But hell, what
can I do? My cover's blown now, if it wasn't when I
got on this overrated bird. I can't order EFs around

205

anymore and expect to be obeyed. And you can hardly expect to succeed by taking me hostage: half those EF shuttles are carrying C.I.D. people. Take me hostage, and they'll blast you. With pleasure."

"You're sure your cover's blown?"

"Wasn't sure before, but, hell. Must've blown it when I helped you get this crate off Newhome's deck."

"Who says you helped?"

"Beg pardon?"

"Who says you helped me? This thing isn't all that hard to fly. Is it totally beyond the realm of possibility that I might have taken it by myself? It's what I meant to do. I have a reputation to uphold here, you know."

"Reputation didn't tell you to keep the converter pressure down."

"You know that, and I know that." I sighed, dimly aware that my reasoning was sound but my explanation wasn't. Reputation couldn't make me think straight, either. "Look, nobody knows what sources of information I might have, or what brilliant flashes of intuition guide me, for space sake. I mean, I've just been listening to a newscaster who has me in the running for God. Don't you think God could steal a Sunfinch without help, if She got a sudden whim to?"

I couldn't find any place to rest my left hand that didn't hurt. After several tries, I settled for balancing the elbow on the edge of the control console, hand in the air. "We don't have a lot of time here. Use your imagination. You're an EF officer. You were hiding in the Sunfinch when I stole it. I overpowered you and took it. During the battle out here you got free, or woke up, or whatever, and now you overpower me. In my current weakened condition, that shouldn't be much of a job. Maybe your cover's blown with the muckymucks out of Newhome, and maybe it isn't; but won't it hold long enough to convince the rabble out from Earth to let us leave this quadrant, particularly if we ask permission to run for Earth? It wouldn't hurt to start our run in that direction. The Sunfinch has a real nice turning radius."

"They'll track us. When we turn—"

"I'll outrun the bastards. Just give me the opening, that's all I ask."

"In your condition, that'll be a job. Even for you. In a Sunfinch."

"Give me the opening. I can do it."

"Skyrider," said the Comm Link. It was Michael's voice, sounding anxious. "Melacha?"

Jake looked at me. "Don't know how much of a head start we'll get. 'Specially if we turn toward Earth, to start."

"If you don't do it, and quickly, I'll just quietly ram this Sunfinch down the nearest Earther's throat. For fun, you know? Hell, I could probably fly my way out of here without your help. I guess I just wanted to do it the easy way, for once."

"You got it," she said abruptly, and reached past me to flip on the Comm Link transmitter. "This is Commander Jacquesmith." Her voice was suddenly businesslike and official, like a real EF commander. "I must apologize for the inconvenience, Pilot Rendell, but I've been obliged to assume control of this barge as of now. No, I wouldn't advise any rash actions; as you can see, I have you in my sights." She had slipped the Sunfinch sideways without effort, almost without thinking, to keep Michael's Starbird under her guns. "I assure you, your relative will be well cared for when we reach an Earth station. In the meantime, please do not attempt to interfere with a C.I.D. shuttle about its lawful business, which this is." I saw her scanning the Earther ships, looking for one she recognized. "Will the ranking C.I.D. officer out here please identify?"

"C.I.D. Minister of Affairs here," said a prim female voice. "Armageddon."

"Ragnarok," said Jake. Formalities thus attended to, the prim voice commanded Jake to report. After a moment's hesitation, she said, "Over the Comm Link, sir?"

"Just the cover," said the voice.

Jake frowned and said carefully, "Routine patrol. Computer malfunction. Sought refuge, Station New-home. Crew overpowered by terrorists. I managed to escape, intending to repair ship's computer and effect crew rescue. Repairs successful. But I . . . before I could . . . I was myself overpowered by the Skyrider, who . . . doubtless mistook me for one of the terrorists."

"Are you not in uniform?" asked the voice, prim-mer than ever.

"I am, sir. However, the Skyrider is not function-ing to full capacity. She has been gravely wounded, sir, presumably while attempting the rescue of the terrorists' hostages. It seemed advisable to seize the ship from her; her mind wanders. Delirium, I think, sir. Request permission to take her to a hospital station soonest, sir."

The prim voice cleared its throat. Michael said again, not hopefully, "Melacha?"

"Sorry, Rendell," said Jake. "I assure you, the Skyrider will receive immediate medical attention. In view of her service, and yours, to the people—"

"Permission granted," said the prim voice.

"Thank you, sir." Jake's voice was sober and serious, but she was grinning like a big black cat that had just lunched on canary. I looked a question at her, and she nodded. That was all I needed. I flipped off the Comm Link transceiver and hit the jockey thrusters, aiming for the nearest hole in the clutter of ships around us. Luckily, the space I aimed for was in the general direction of Earth; I really wasn't thinking very clearly. I'd have aimed for any space I saw, and if it hadn't been in the right direction, old Prim Voice would have had half the EFs on our tail in a minute. As it was, I could feel them watching as we skittered somewhat unsteadily in toward the sun. It reminded me that I'd damn well better think clearly, if I wanted to get out of this mess alive. Prim Voice could still catch us, if I didn't keep my eye on her and her Earther colleagues.

"If you give it another ten minutes toward Earth," Jake suggested.

I shook my head, which was a mistake. It took me nearly a full minute to chase back the dizzying darkness, and I reminded myself not to make any further such rash movements. "I don't have ten minutes," I said.

"If you turn sooner . . ."

"I can outfly and outshoot any damn thing they throw at me."

She gave me an odd look. "You believe your own PR."

"Somebody has to." I looked at her. "If I wait till we hit your mark, and then turn there, can you guarantee they won't spot us?"

"Course not. 'Fraid they still might."

"And if they do, can you outfly or outshoot them?"

She wanted to say yes. After a moment she said, "Anything but the Sunfinches."

"Okay. I can do it to the Sunfinches. But it's got to be now." I swung our own Sunfinch in a deep, steep curve, hoping I'd allowed myself enough distance, and knowing I couldn't wait for more. Reality was fading in and out again, dark on light, stars on shadows, and I wasn't sure I hadn't pushed it too far already.

Back at Station Newhome, both fleets had figured out my maneuver by now. The Colonial frequency light on the Comm Link was blinking at me. I took time to punch it open, wordlessly. Michael's voice said distantly, "Don't be a hero."

I tried to laugh, but it didn't come out quite right. "Don't start a war." I hoped they were all listening. This was important, though I couldn't quite recall why. "You hear me? Whether or not I get away with this is none of your damn business. This is my baby. Your job is over, for today. All of you. We damn near had the war started over this already, and instead we fought together, and by God if anybody starts it now, after all the trouble I've gone to, I'll personally kill the son of a bitch."

Somebody else laughed, more successfully than I had. "We hear you, Skyrider. Don't worry about us. Just get safely home with that new malite converter, okay?"

"Okay." My voice sounded distant and dreamy. Probably nobody but Jake heard it, anyway; we were nearly out of Comm range. All the EF shuttles had fallen behind, except the Sunfinches. There were three of those, and they had guessed my intentions—not all that difficult a task at this point—and headed to cut me off.

"If my cover wasn't blown, it is now," said Jake.

"Does it matter?"

"Relief, in a way. If we survive this flight."

"We'll survive it."

"Confidence, or bravado?"

I was beginning to like Jake. "Some of each. You want the percentages?"

"Percentages?"

"You know. How much of each."

"Oh." She studied me a moment. "No, thanks."

"Wise choice." The EF Sunfinches were ready for me, positioned in a neat triangle that effectively blocked my path—or would have, if I were an ordinary pilot with an ordinary shuttle under me. They were all three riding backward, keeping their firepower trained on me, and cautiously letting me close the gap.

At first I thought they'd just blast me as I went through. They could have, if they'd wanted to. Maybe they thought I'd chicken out. I didn't. But neither did I fire on them. I could have got one or more of them, and the reasons I didn't weren't all political. I didn't want to start a war, of course; but, more important, I didn't want to start a battle I couldn't win. I doubted my ability to take all three of them, unless they got an irrational urge to stand still for target practice. And I guess I half hoped, when they saw they couldn't stop me unless they were willing to kill me, that they'd give up and let me go.

I dived at maximum thrust for the center of their triangle, trusting my guess that however much practice their pilots had had with Sunfinches, they still didn't really believe what a Sunfinch with a crazy pilot could do. It was a good guess. We went through so fast, they didn't know we were coming till we were going. Then they flipped fast enough, I'll give them that, and one of them singed my tail with a snap-shot laser even as he went into a power dive after me. It didn't seem to do any real damage to my Sunfinch, but it shook me. I'd hoped they wouldn't think that fast.

In a flat-out race, they could cling to my tail all the way to Mars; and before we got there, one of them was bound to get lucky with his lasers. Either they were reluctant to blow one of their precious Sunfinches right out of space, or none of them was very good at aiming, but they'd change their minds or improve with practice. Or I'd get too tired to keep ahead of them. The jockeyjuice was a wistful memory now, and I was getting clumsy.

"I'd give my right glove for a flurry of wild rocks about now," I said.

"What for?" asked Jake.

"To dodge. I could. They couldn't."

"Not so sure you could, either." When I looked at her, she added, "In your condition."

"Damn my condition. I'd still give my right glove for the chance to try."

"Enjoying this, aren't you?"

"I'd be enjoying it more if we were out in the Belt. I don't suppose this crate comes equipped with emergency first aid supplies? I could use some jockeyjuice."

She opened a compartment and took out a first aid kit. "Kill you for sure."

"Maybe. It's a better risk than the EFs."

"Could just flip and fire. Seem to be a better shot than they are. Now we're up to speed, we can travel as fast backward as frontward."

"I'll do it if I have to, but I'd rather not kill them. I don't think I'll much like war."

"What's war to do with it?"

"It's what I'd be starting."

"They think I'm flying this bucket." She unwrapped the jockeyjuice hypospray and held it, looking at me.

"I doubt if they think that now, if they ever really did. Besides, that's irrelevant. I don't think I'll like war, no matter who starts it, or who thinks who starts it. In general, I'm just not right fond of killing. It's a queer Belter trait I have. I've done too damn much killing already today. Are you going to give me that thing, or sit there and play with it?"

She looked at it doubtfully. "Kill you quicker'n anything." But she handed it to me. "What'll I do?"

"If I die? Hell, I don't care. I'll be dead." I aimed the thing clumsily, one-handed, at my thigh, and depressed the plunger. The darkness receded. "Anyway, I ain't dead yet."

"May be, soon. They're gaining on us."

I glanced at the scanners. "That doesn't make sense. We're as fast as they are." But they were gaining on us. "What the hell?"

"Blow their damn gaskets," said Jake. "They're revving up the converters past tolerance. Damn it, I've *told* them—"

One of the trailing ships suddenly lost speed and began to fall behind. "You mean they're going to put themselves out of action for me?"

"One did." We watched the scanners as the other two ships slowed back down to my speed again. The one that had slowed first was falling farther behind; the other two seemed content, for the time being, to keep pace with me. "One oh two blew a gasket, for sure. Wonder if they've got anybody aboard who knows how to clean up the mess? Hope to hell they had their shielding up.''

''A minute ago you wanted me to flip and fire on them. Now you worry about their shielding?''

She made a wry face. ''Been with them a long time. Loyalties aren't exactly divided—been working for the Colonies the whole time—but, hell. Some of those guys are my friends.''

It wasn't a problem with which I was wholly unfamiliar. I didn't say anything; I just floated in my seat, enjoying the borrowed strength the jockeyjuice had given me. The pain wasn't gone, but I could cope with it. The main problem now was to get out of the parade.

Out of curiosity, I touched a jockey thruster and watched the trailing ships fall behind as they were slow to correct their courses. When they'd got on my path again, they were just discernibly farther behind, and we were all traveling at top speed. I jockeyed again, and they fell behind a little more on the curve. But when I did it a third time, they didn't follow.

''Not as dumb as they look,'' said Jake. ''Know you're headed for Mars. Jockey all you like, but you'll have to come back on line sometime. If they keep course for Mars, they'll be ahead of you if you keep this up.''

''An interesting thought.'' I was edging right out of scanner range to one side, wondering whether they would have the nerve to let me go. They hadn't, the first time, or the second; but on the third try they gave it up and headed straight for Mars again. ''That's done it,'' I said.

''Done what?''

''I've lost them.''

"Told you. Angle back for Mars and you'll've lost time. Find them there before you."

"They'll certainly get to Mars before me, if they're going to Mars. I'm not."

"You're what?"

"I'm not going to Mars. What d'you think I am, some kind of heroic idiot? I wanted a Falcon, or at least a Starbird, for my wingmate, and damned if I think Earth's going to give me it now that I've stolen a Sunfinch. So I'll have to get it somewhere else. Did you think I was going to hand over a valuable Sunfinch to the Colonials out of the goodness of my heart or something? They can afford a Falcon, for space sake."

"You'd *sell* her? Whose side are you on, anyway?"

"Mine." I looked at her speculatively. "D'you think you want to try to stop me?"

She thought about it. Probably she thought she could, when the jockeyjuice wore off. Meantime, she knew damn well she couldn't, and after a moment she laughed. "Hell, no. It's your show, Skyrider."

CHAPTER TWENTY-TWO

Fortunately, we didn't have to go all the way to the Belt, or even to Mars. I never would have made it. The second dose of jockeyjuice hadn't killed me, but a third might have done the job. It wasn't an experiment I really wanted to try.

However, Jamin and Michael knew me a little better than did the EFs who were taking their Sunfinches to Mars to wait for me. Jamin had long since dropped off his extraneous passengers, and apparently had made it back to the battle lines in time to watch me make my escape. He and Michael got together and plotted my probable course—accurately enough for me to find it a little scary, later on, when I learned what had happened—and drew aside a couple of Colonial high muckymucks to whom they explained their assessment of the situation. They didn't have to guess what I wanted; I'd told them that, when we first set out for Station Newhome.

The Colonials were delighted with the opportunity

to trade a mere Falcon for a Sunfinch. Michael and
Jamin didn't strike a very good bargain; the Sunfinch
was worth a hell of a lot more than that. Still, I'd
have liked to watch the negotiations. Both Michael
and Jamin disapproved of my mercenary tendencies,
and there they were, doing my bargaining for me. It
was Collis who had sense enough to ask for a life-of-
the-vessel maintenance guarantee. He knew the deal
I'd made with the Company when I earned my Falcon, and he'd been around me long enough to lose
some of the suicidal altruistic values with which Jamin
tried to instill him.

They commandeered a pair of Falcons from the
Colonial Fleet, and set out for the coordinates at
which they hoped to find me, on my way to the Belt.
I don't know how they convinced the Colonials that
the chance of finding me there was adequate to justify the expenditure of fuel. Perhaps, as Jamin was
always so fond of telling me, my reputation really
did precede me. Maybe the Colonials were smart
enough to figure out that the Skyrider wasn't the sort
of woman to risk her life stealing a Sunfinch just so
she could give it away. Though really, considering
that all I got in return for it was Jamin's Falcon,
that's just about what I did.

At the time, I was in no condition to quibble. The
second dose of jockeyjuice was almost worn off, and
Jake was almost as well aware of it as I was. We
both knew I couldn't last much longer without another dose of the stuff or prompt medical attention;
and we both knew I probably couldn't survive another dose.

The second one had used up all the reserves I had.
That's what jockeyjuice does. It doesn't give you
anything you haven't got. It just gives access to

everything you have. If you use up what stored energy your body is holding in reserve, and take more jockeyjuice in hope of keeping up your energy level after that, what happens is that your poor overworked system tries to keep going on nothing at all. In order to be as effective as it is in times of stress, the stuff uses up a body's resources at several times the normal rate, but that's not something you really notice—till you take one dose too many. Then you tend to die.

I was thinking of trying it anyway. Jake was trying to think how to talk me out of it. She was also trying to figure out how to grab the Sunfinch and triumphantly deliver it into Colonial care, with or without my consent and assistance, but I wasn't supposed to know that.

Well, maybe that would be the best thing that could happen, at this point. Maybe this time I had overestimated my own abilities. Maybe I had been a little too ready to believe my own PR. Or maybe I'd just been too damn childishly thrilled with the notion of stealing a Sunfinch right out from under the Company's collective nose. Whatever the cause, I had taken enough wrong turns and made enough bad guesses that the chances of my survival were slim and getting slimmer.

It wasn't like me to pull something quite this stupid. The initial theft, yes; there'd been an element of danger and defiance in that, too strong for me to resist. And after that, the determination that Colonials should have the thing and that I should extract some payment for bringing it to them was perfectly reasonable and in character for me. Michael had said that the Colonies needed the new malite conversion drive to win the war Earth was pushing us into, but I could hardly hand it over for free. I did have a reputation to maintain.

I had risked my life for that often enough, and for less; the risk of my life wasn't what bothered me. The problem was that I had set this one up so stupidly, there was hardly any risk of my *survival*. And that didn't make sense. I like living. I'm happiest, it's true, when I can pit my skills against the universe, any way it happens, just for the thrill of cheating Death; but where's the thrill in dying? It's something we all have to try, someday, but why hurry? It'll wait.

I kept thinking I must have missed something. When we left the battle scene back at Newhome, I must have had some plan in mind that I'd since forgotten, confused as I was by pain and drugs and fatigue. There must be something about the situation that I was missing. Because it looked as though I would have to choose between keeping the Sunfinch, or keeping my life. If I turned back to Earth or Mars, where I could get medical attention, I would lose the Sunfinch. If I kept on toward the Belt, I knew I couldn't make it, and then it became a question of just how badly Jake really wanted the Sunfinch; when I collapsed, she would have to choose between going on with it, or turning back for me.

Logically, since so many lives would eventually depend on Colonial mastery of the new malite converter, the Sunfinch was worth a hell of a lot more than my life. But I was afraid Jake wouldn't be good enough at math to see that. People so often decide that the life they're standing next to is of greater value than half a dozen or even half a hundred or more lives at a distance. She just might get stupid and turn back toward Earth in an effort to save me.

And I couldn't figure out how I'd got myself into a situation like that. I really don't volunteer for suicide missions. Maybe I needed a psych-tender. Or maybe I had needed one, at the start of this journey. I wasn't going to need much of anything, at the end of it. Since I couldn't trust Jake to take the Sunfinch to the Colonials while I was alive, the only logical move was to try another jolt of jockeyjuice. If it killed me, Jake would be free to take the Sunfinch on out to the Belt or Mars. If it didn't kill me, I would have another shot at getting the damn thing out there myself.

It seemed logical at the time. Maybe the previous doses of jockeyjuice had scrambled my brain. Anyway, I had another dose in my hand, ready to use, when I scanned three Falcons and a Starbird in our path.

Jake was busy telling me all the reasons I should put the jockeyjuice away and let her take me back to Earth for the med-techs. I put the hypospray aside, forgetting it would float off when I let go of it, and punched the forward scanners up to maximum magnification. We were still too far away; I couldn't determine the shuttles' origin. "Damn it," I said, wondering which of my many wrong guesses was turning up now. Had the EFs figured out where to look for me? But it wasn't Sunfinches. Had they sent the Patrol? We were too far from the Belt—or from any other habitation—for the Patrol to have happened upon us by accident.

"Damn what?" Jake caught the floating hypospray before she looked at the screens. "Oh. Who in space . . . ?"

Belatedly, I noticed the Comm Link blinking at me. I had left the transceiver turned clear off, so all

they could do was signal their desire to communicate.
I still didn't figure out that I was looking at the
missing factor in my plans. I just stupidly punched
on the Comm Link and said, "Identify." I meant to
sound crisp and official, but I missed it by a long
shot.

"*Defiance*," said Jamin's voice.

"What in space are you doing out here?"

"Waiting for you. Do you think you can dock that
thing with a Falcon?"

There it was in words, and I still didn't know what
I had. "No way. I didn't bring it out here to give it
away."

A different voice said, diffidently, "We were told
you might accept a Falcon in trade."

"She needs medical attention," said Jake.

"You keep out of this," I said.

"If you can dock with it, it's yours," said Michael.

"What is?" I asked stupidly.

"That Falcon you asked for."

"How did you find me?"

"An exercise in illogic," said Jamin. "We tried to
think like you. Then we just got here first, which was
easy, since we could take a direct course while you
were jockeying all over the System to lose those
EFs."

"Can't dock with anything," said Jake. "She's
half dead. Needs med-techs, I said."

"I can dock with anything," I said. "Which one?"

"Take your choice," said the stranger's voice that
had spoken before. "The one to starboard of the
Defiance is of more recent manufacture, but the one
to port is more heavily armed. Both are in top condition, and both pilots know how to fly that overgrown
dragonfly you're riding. At least, we think we can. If

it has any eccentricities about which we should be warned, we trust you'll let us know?"

"I can fly it home for you," said Jake. "You better get the Skyrider back to Earth orbit. She's not fit to fly."

"To hell with that," I said, frowning at the two Falcons flanking the *Defiance*. "I'll take the one to port, if that's all right with you, Jamin? It is your shuttle, after all."

"That's the one I wanted. Engage synch systems." He sounded more relieved than the decision warranted. It wasn't until much later that I realized his relief was at the prospect of getting me safely off the Sunfinch and into the med-techs' care.

"Give it a minute," I said. "How did you say you found me?"

"Dock it, Melacha," said Michael. "We'll talk about it later."

"No, I want to know now." It seemed important. I was beginning to realize this was the missing element I'd been looking for, but I didn't understand it.

"We're friends," said Jamin, summing it up rather nicely. "We've been together a while, now. It wasn't that hard to figure out what you'd do. We plotted a likely course, and here we are. Now will you dock that thing before you lose it?"

"I'm not about to lose it. I'm just fine, thank you." It wasn't true, but we heroic types are supposed to say that.

"Just dock it," said Michael.

I docked it. The procedure was simple, really; our ships' computers did it for us. There was a hairy moment when my hand slipped, but the computer corrected nicely, and the docking hooks slid home with a reassuring click.

I didn't complete the transfer from one ship to another; the jockeyjuice wore off. They told me afterward that Jake, Michael, and the spare Falcon headed out for the Belt with the Sunfinch while Jamin flew my *Defiance* back to Earth orbit beside his new Falcon, whose pilot had willingly stayed on board when Jake dragged me feet-first through the hatch.

There was some initial confusion, apparently, over Jake's shiny EF uniform, but judicial use of Colonial code words cleared that up fairly quickly. She helped strap me into the hammock in the pilot's quarters of Jamin's new Falcon, made a few choice remarks about unprintable hero types, and went back to disengage the Sunfinch a lot more smoothly than I'd docked it.

I didn't know anything about it. I didn't know anything about anything, for a while. Which was something of a relief, actually.

CHAPTER TWENTY-THREE

Officially, the government hadn't the smallest concern over my theft of the Sunfinch. Not everyone
was quite happy about it, of course; but the deed was
accomplished, and apparently somebody figured out
that the smartest thing to do about it at that point was
to keep quiet. Which should have meant my job was
over, mission accomplished, everything all wrapped
up and hardly even a bow left to tie. Unfortunately, it
didn't quite work out that way.

We were back at the same freefall station from
which the hostages had originally been snatched. The
med-techs had put my leg back together, and got my
hand healed to the point where they were beginning
to lay plans for rebuilding it. Modern medical technology being what it is, none of that had taken a
great deal of time, once I was in reach of the proper
facilities. One day they're going to invent some kind
of convenient portable healer: a handy little medical
gadget that fits in the pocket of a flight suit and

mends everything from hangnails to laser chars in no time flat, leaving the heroic warrior to carry on about his business without these pesky side trips to Sick Bay. Or maybe they won't. It would put a lot of med-techs out of a job.

The ones working on me were having a lot more fun than I was. They examined the remains of my hand from every angle through every conceivable examination device, and discussed the possibilities with each other and with me in interminable detail, with the rather startling enthusiasm common to people in their profession whenever they're confronted with what they regard as an interesting case.

I just wanted the hand fixed. I kept telling them that, and they kept describing all the available methods and options, none of which I really wanted to know about. I realize that some people like to get personally involved in their own medical care, and I think I understand the impulse. I can even imagine situations in which I would feel the same way. This was not one of them. My hand could be fixed, or it couldn't. There were different ways to try it, and I didn't understand a damn thing about any of them, even when they had been explained a few times. I figured it was the med-techs' job to choose the best method and use it; and my job to live with the results, whatever they were.

I was handing out that little speech two or three times an hour, it seemed, and I had just delivered it to yet another med-tech in response to yet another incomprehensible medical summary, when the first indication came in that only the fun part of my job was over. There was still work to be done.

Collis brought me the news. He'd had time, apparently, to get sufficiently accustomed to the peculiarities of life in freefall that the thrill was gone. He wasn't bouncing off walls anymore. He wasn't bouncing off anything, any more than he had to, to get where he was going. He floated almost sedately to my hammockside, put his arm through a handhold, and greeted me rather diffidently.

"Are you all right, Collis?" I asked.

His gaze flicked nervously toward the med-tech on my other side, and away again. "I'm fine," he said firmly. "Haven't they fixed your hand yet?"

"Not completely. It's healed enough to live with, but it won't do me much good till they rebuild some of the muscle."

"As I have said before," said the med-tech, "the problem is not only the muscles. There is considerable old damage to the bone structure—"

I grinned ruefully at Collis. "They're always on about how often I break my knuckles on other people's jaws. How's the rest of the world getting along without me?"

"They keep canceling the summit meeting."

"They what!"

"Papa said not to bother you about it, 'specially since they've agreed to go on with it again, now. There's nothing you could do, anyway, he says."

"What seems to be the problem?"

He produced a boyish expression of disdain. "Oh, you know. Just all the same old stuff. The Earthers don't believe anything, and the Colonists can't prove anything, and everybody's cross all the time."

"What is it that the Earthers don't believe and we can't prove, this time?"

"Oh, the *Marabou*, and the terrorists, you know." He sighed. "Skyrider, there's going to be a war, isn't there?"

I might have produced the easy lie for a different six-year-old, but I owed Collis better than that. He wouldn't have believed the lie anyway. "I'm afraid so. The only real question is when."

"Why, though? Nobody really wants it, do they?"

"Not really, I don't think. But sometimes we're too stubborn or too stupid to do what we really want. Don't worry about it; we'll get back to the Belt before it happens. And now that you and your father can share quarters, we'll all be okay. That'll be one thing less for him to worry about, anyway." The part about us being okay wasn't a lie, exactly. It was just undue optimism. But something about what I'd said bothered Collis. I couldn't tell exactly what it was, and he wouldn't say. He wanted to talk about the summit meeting, instead.

"Couldn't you talk to them, Skyrider? You chased the fake Colonials away from the *Marabou*, and you saw the fake terrorists, and even stole their Sunfinch, and everything. Couldn't you tell them?"

"I have told them. But I can't prove a damn thing, and why should they believe me? The people behind the war effort are mostly muckymucks, with damn good stories to explain away mine, and a lot more credibility with the public—on both sides of the issues—than a battered old Belter like me could ever have."

"What's credibility?"

"It means people believe them."

"Oh."

The med-tech, whom both of us had been ignoring, made a sound that might have passed for laughter in some circles. "Why don't you tell the boy the truth?" she asked bitterly. "You certainly don't have to maintain your stupid lies for my sake. I can't influence anybody, even if you could convince me, which you can't, because I know what really happened.''

Collis and I both looked at her in surprise. ''I give up,'' I said. ''What really happened?''

''You created both incidents. You Colonials, with all your mutants and halfbreeds, with God knows what motives, maybe just for the fun of it, maybe because monsters enjoy war, I don't know, but I do know my son died in the last war, and I hope you get what you're asking for, I hope you get your war, I hope all the real humans on Earth band together and wipe out every last mutant and misfit in space.''

This, from a med-tech. I said mildly, ''There was a time in the last century or two when the 'real' humans weren't fully convinced that people with your skin pigmentation qualified as human.''

''History has nothing to do with this,'' she said with marvelous illogic.

Well, there wasn't much I could say to that. ''Go away,'' I said finally. ''If there's a mutant med-tech on this station, send him to me, and we'll talk about rebuilding my hand. Otherwise, I'm checking out, now. I don't want treatment from anyone medically ignorant enough to refer to me as a halfbreed.''

''We do not employ mutant med-techs on this station.'' She sounded proud of that.

''I'll be leaving, then.'' I unfastened the straps that held me in the hammock. I was becoming adept at performing simple tasks one-handed. ''Thanks very much for all your assistance.'' I floated out of the hammock and looked back at her. I'm not particularly proud of what I said then, but I've never been noted for my even temper. I think I did well not to knock her teeth down her throat. "In a way, it's lucky your son did die in the last war, isn't it?"

She stared at me, shocked and maybe a little frightened, and didn't ask what I meant.

I told her anyway. "Things being how they are, these days, it's perfectly possible that, had he lived, he might have married one of them."

Her mouth opened, but it took a moment for the sound to come out. "My son? Marry a *mutant?*"

"A fate worse than death, surely." I took Collis's hand and we got out of there, before I could change my mind about rearranging her face just a little. She looked as though she thought her son really was better off dead. A face like that could use a little rearranging.

Collis didn't say anything till we were in the corridor with the Sick Bay door safely shut behind us. "But will your hand be all right? It looks . . ." He hesitated, and looked anxiously at my face. "I mean . . ."

"It looks like hell, I know." It looked more like a claw than a hand, with very little flesh to cover the bones, and much of that synthetic. "It'll do, till I can get back to the Belt." And if I knew Belter medtechs (which I ought to, by now), there wouldn't be any nonsense about choices and methods. There would be fixing. There would be a lot of complaining, of course; they were tired, at Home Base, of mending my hands and the jaws my hands had collided with. But they didn't consider Floaters and Fallers less than human. "Now what's all this about the summit meeting?"

"Somebody called it off," said Collis. "I think it as the Earthers; they didn't like it that the whole

Colonial Fleet showed up at Newhome. There isn't
supposed to be a Colonial Fleet anymore."

"What changed their minds about calling it off?"

"Mostly Board Advisor Brown."

"I can believe that. D'you know how she did it?"

"No. I'm not supposed to be at the meetings.
They're boring anyway."

"Which means you've been to one or more, or
you wouldn't know that, right?"

He gave me one of his angelic, inscrutable smiles,
and looked away. I thought his face looked paler than
it should; but then, he'd been through a lot lately.
We all had. "See, I was just playing. I didn't even
know that was where they were going to have their
dumb old meeting. And when they started coming in,
well, kind of I thought I s'pose I should've left, but
they were already talking when they came in, these
two first ones, and I thought they were talking about
your shuttle because they said that name, you know,
the *Defiance*, they were saying something about that,
and I wanted to hear if it was your shuttle, and then
it was too late because some more came in and
everything."

"Where's your father?"

"At the meeting, I think."

"Good. Let's go there. What did these two say
about defiance?"

"Something about the Colonial Fleet was it. Open
defiance, they said."

"D'you know who they were?"

"Just two old Earthers, I don't know. I'd know
them if I saw them again, I guess. They kind of
scared me. Skyrider, what's a sashanater?"

"*What?*"

"Well, they talked about it," he said defensively.

"About somebody condoning open defiance, and then about this sashanater. It sounded like a job, you know? Like putting away all your things, or something, because they didn't want to do it and they were going to get Colonials to do it for them."

"What exactly did you hear, Collis?"

"Well, the woman was mad at the man. I guess because he didn't do his jobs right. I don't know what his jobs were, though, they didn't say. And the woman kept saying nothing worked, and something about the Colonial Fleet coming out like that, it was an act of open defiance, that's what she said, and that somebody condoned it, I didn't hear who, maybe the Board of Directors, or something, it sounded like somebody important, you know? And, I don't know, they used big words and it was all confused, but then they said about the sashanater. How if the Colonials did that, it would work for sure."

"Can you remember their exact words, Collis? This may be important."

"Um." He grasped a handhold, thinking hard. "About the sashanater? Well, um. 'We've put up with that woman long enough. She stands,' um, I forget, in the way or something, I think they said her heart bleeds. She must be awful sick, huh? Then, um, something something 'Colonials asashanater we'll have our war.' " He looked at me for approval. "Is that good?"

"Collis, was the word 'assassinate'? Did they say they would 'assassinate her'?"

His face brightened. "That's it. What's it mean, Skyrider?"

"I'm not just sure."

He was thinking about something else already, or

that answer would hardly have satisfied him. "They wanted war, didn't they?"

"It sounds like."

"The President doesn't want war. She said so, and I believe her, she was nice to me, but she's supposed to be in charge and everything, so why do the Earthers keep trying to make war if she doesn't want it?"

"She doesn't know everything they do," I said, and paused, and stared at him. "She said so? She was nice to you? You've met her?"

"Sure, we were playing Planets, she's got the neatest electronic board, lots better than mine. I met her in the rec room."

"When was this?"

He didn't seem to find anything unusual in the idea of consorting with presidents. "Before breakfast. I got up and nobody else was and Papa had said I could go to the rec room when I wanted to, once when he just didn't want to talk to me. *She* said I was lots more fun to talk to than most of her aides. D'you think she really meant it? Because I like her."

"I expect she meant it. Did you tell her anything about what you've just told me?"

"No. We just talked about Planets." He thought about it. "Oh, and about you a little."

"About me?"

"Yeah. She wanted to know about you and the *Marabou* and the terrorists and all that. I told her my dad's a war hero, too. I told her some of the stuff he did in the war. And we talked about Board Advisor Brown, I guess. Because it was the President who told me it was Board Advisor Brown who kept the summit meeting from breaking up."

"You seem to've had quite a chat."

"We did. But then she had to go to work and I

thought Papa might wonder about me but he didn't so that's when I came to see you. After breakfast, of course.''

"Of course." I guess it's as well to know where one fits in the scheme of things.

CHAPTER TWENTY-FOUR

Strictly speaking, of course, my job description didn't include assassination prevention, no matter who was the target. And as a loyal Colonial, maybe I shouldn't have cared very much what happened to Earth's officials, elected or otherwise. But of course I wasn't, strictly speaking, a loyal Colonial. As I made a point of reminding folks at frequent intervals, I wasn't in the habit of displaying loyalty to anyone but me. I was a mercenary, plain and simple. And if there were anything more potentially profitable than preventing the assassination of the President of the whole World, Incorporated, I'd have liked to know what it was.

I don't claim profit was my only motive for leaping so steadfastly to the aid of the president of a government for which I had very little liking. Greed has always been a strong motivator for me, but there were other factors involved. Curiosity was one. I had wanted to know, when I helped bring in the *Marabou* with all her passengers intact, who on Earth wanted war so badly that he, she, or it would go to such lengths to get one started. I never had found out, and I still wanted to know.

Of course there was no particular reason to believe that there was any connection between the conversation Collis had overheard, even if we had correctly interpreted what he heard, and the sabotage of the *Marabou*. But how many people could there be with the political pull to have not only a passenger liner, but also the military rescue effort and the private shuttle that went out after her, all sabotaged? All under the watchful eyes of the Patrol? Or to send out, as a last effort when I'd spaced all their other attempts to kill us, a squadron of fake Colonial Warriors with Patrol insignia showing under their hastily contrived Colonial Fleet paint jobs? Or to convince a lot of otherwise sensible Earther officials that the holofilms presented in evidence of that battle, and the reports of numerous witnesses afterward, were so much rockdust contrived by rabid Insurrectionists?

The person who had that political pull might also have the power to set up a secret government agency whose purpose was the same as that of the *Marabou* incident: war, between Earth and her Colonies, with the Colonies cast in the role of the evil aggressors. I don't know whether PR has always been as important a factor in war as it is in modern times, but I do know that these days it's just about the deciding factor.

Somebody was trying to destroy our image. Most people on both sides were glad enough to remain at peace, however precarious that peace might be. Most of us realized that war was probably inevitable, but we weren't in a hurry; we were willing to let things

take their natural course, and hope for the best.
Probably the only real question, as I'd told Collis,
was not whether, but when war would break out
again: and whose public image would survive most
nearly intact. Somebody was pushing. I wanted to
know who.

The conversation Collis had overheard was the
closest thing I'd had to a clue in a while. Admittedly,
it was dubious. It would have been more dubious if
Collis were less bright, but I knew this kid. If he said
the word was assassination, it was. And in the con-
text in which he had heard it, it sure as hell sounded
like Presidential assassination. It was worth looking
into, anyway.

The first step was to get Collis to point out to me
the two people whose conversation he had overheard.
I had even fewer doubts, after that. I sent him away,
and took up a neutral position in the meeting chamber, ostensibly to listen to the proceedings, and studied the two people he had indicated.

One of them was a florid Earther gentleman in a
conservative suit, with sandy hair and bushy eyebrows and great wet brown eyes that never really
stopped to look at anything because they were too
busy scanning the whole chamber with a nervous
little frown. If I'd had to guess his occupation, I'd
have said attorney or insurance salesman, or maybe
politician. He was probably a spy. It wasn't of much
importance, because I knew for sure what the other
one did for a living.

She had been introduced to me by Board Advisor
Brown, seemingly a long time ago, back before Mi-
chael and Jamin and I had made the flight out to
Station Newhome. She was still wearing her neat
C.I.D. uniform and the faintest hint of a superior

smile on the face I'd wanted to rearrange. Now and
then, as she listened to the proceedings, she lifted an
elegant eyebrow and whispered something amused
and possibly deadly to the florid insurance salesman
at her side. I wondered what he called her, if he ever
addressed her by name. Probably not McCormick,
but that was the only name she had given us.

I didn't really care what she called herself. Right
now I was a lot more concerned with her plans than
with her name. I glanced at the others in the room,
wondering whether she had found time to implement
her homicidal impulses, and didn't see any Earthers
masquerading as Colonials. That was a good sign,
though not conclusive; real Colonials could be fooled
or bought.

The politician who'd been speaking when I entered
droned on interminably. The President seemed to be
interested in what he was saying. She was strapped,
Earther-fashion, into a chair at one end of the chamber, facing all the other muckymucks. She seemed
oblivious to the fact that she couldn't have presented
a better target to anybody who hadn't come just to
listen to political doubletalk delivered with more force
than coherence. Maybe it wouldn't have been politic
for her to employ a personnel shield for herself at a
summit meeting, but she could at least have selected
a less well lighted, isolated, indefensible area to sit
in.

I didn't even notice her personal bodyguards, the
Special Service folks, at first, because they were so
uselessly deployed at such a distance from her. They
didn't look any happier about the situation than I
would have been in their place. I suppose when you
work for the President you do what she tells you,
even when what she tells you means, in effect, that

you won't be able to do your job. The only reason I spotted them at all was that I was looking for assassins; and that's essentially what a bodyguard is, or had best be prepared to be.

The assassin in whom I was particularly interested, however, would probably not be wearing a Special Service uniform. There were three of those, and I marked their locations carefully in my mind while I searched the remainder of the crowd. If anything interesting did occur, those three would involve themselves one way or another, and I wouldn't want to get in their line of fire.

If I'd had anything more to go on than a six-year-old's somewhat confusing report, I might have taken what I knew or suspected to the proper authorities and let the Special Service people protect the President; it was their job, not mine. But even if Collis had heard a detailed assassination plot and reported it to me verbatim, the Special Service might well have disregarded my repetition of it. People too frequently disregard or at least underestimate children. Especially Earthers, whose offspring mature so slowly, if at all. The Special Service didn't, of course, employ Colonials.

The C.I.D., as represented by McCormick, was less fastidious. I knew, when I finally spotted her assassin, that he hadn't been bought; he was the sort of man who couldn't be bought. But he could very easily be fooled. Poor Garrett, the hot-headed Company pilot who had made remarks about my loyalties, and nearly lost his head for it. He wasn't any more difficult to spot than he was to fool: he was the most nervous person present. He fancied himself quite an adventurer, the Great White Hunter variety, or maybe the mysterious Secret Agent on a Mission. But he'd

never really killed anyone before. McCormick had
found time to implement her plans, but she hadn't,
apparently, examined the record of the first seemingly appropriate tool that came to hand.

I did look over the rest of the crowd rather carefully, just to be sure; Garrett seemed altogether too
easy, like being given a puzzle and its solution all in
the same package. He could have been a decoy. But
he wasn't. There wasn't anyone else in the chamber
who hadn't legitimate business there, and none of
them considered assassination to be legitimate business, that day. I'd have recognized the look, if any of
them had it. Very few sane humans can prepare to assassinate a fellow human without some sign of it showing
in their manner or at least in their eyes. A certain
bleak—or sometimes feverish—determination. . . .

Garrett had it. The feverish variety. And he had
the weapon. That alone was a giveaway, and I was
surprised the Special Service people hadn't picked up
on it. Colonials were forbidden by law to carry lethal
handguns. That we were allowed to carry handguns
at all was a concession bitterly won, and openly
despised by supposedly civilized Earthers, who had
no use for handguns in their daily lives.

Neither had we, ordinarily, but we weren't as far
from our frontier past as the Earthers were. We
didn't often use them, but by God we wanted the
right to wear them, and wear them we did, everywhere we went. Even into a summit meeting chamber. Which might have explained the Special Service
people's failure to notice that Garrett's gun was lethal. They might have been so bothered by all the
handguns strapped so casually to so many Colonial
hips that they wouldn't even notice that one of the
many was a laser, not a stun gun. At any rate, they

hadn't noticed. And I was at the opposite end of the chamber from the weapon in question: not a convenient location from which to do anything about it.

There were several ways I could have handled it. There was time to consider, and discard, several possibilities. That I didn't waste time cursing McCormick's efficiency was due primarily to the fact that the thought didn't occur to me until much later. The important thing right then was to prevent Garrett from starting the war I'd been at such pains to put off for a while. As a secondary but very attractive goal, I thought it would be satisfying to involve McCormick in the resolution of the nasty little problem she had posed.

If she had hired a real assassin, I would have had to handle it quite differently. But I knew Garrett, and I thought I knew in a general way what was going on in his not altogether capable mind. I hoped I knew how he would react to certain stimuli. In fact, I was counting on it.

McCormick was almost as easy to second-guess, though for different reasons. She was cleverer than Garrett, but she wasn't nearly as clever as she thought she was. And, more important, she wasn't as courageous as she liked to pretend. If she were, she'd have done some of her dirty work herself, instead of fobbing it off onto fools and incompetents and (that least dependable servant of all) Chance.

It was time to make my move. The politician who'd been speaking showed signs of running down; and Garrett had by now had ample time to psych himself up to his task if he could. There would probably be a general aimless stirring and shifting throughout the chamber when the politician finally shut up, and that would be the time for Garrett to act

242 Melisa C. Michaels

if he was going to. I couldn't get to him in time, but I could get to McCormick.

She saw me coming, but she wasn't expecting trouble. She awarded me a cool nod of recognition as I slipped into place behind her. Using her body to shield me from the watchful eyes of the Special Service people, I drew my stun gun and pressed its muzzle hard against her back. It would have been very poor technique with a fighter—guns are for shooting, not for poking, and people who use them for poking me will get disarmed in such a hurry they won't know what happened—but she wasn't a fighter. My free hand was useless, but the arm worked fine, so I put it over her shoulder with the forearm resting against her neck to keep us from floating apart. She stiffened and started to turn toward me as realization came to her that all was not well between us.

"Maintain," I suggested pleasantly. "The weapon at your back is a laser. At this angle, I expect it would perforate your liver quite satisfactorily. The med-techs are so incompetent about rebuilding livers, and transplants are always in short supply. Maybe you'd best call off your dog before my finger gets tired of not pulling the firing button."

She had more guts than I'd given her credit for. "I don't know what you're talking about." Her voice was level and cool.

"You'd better figure it out before something untoward happens. If the President dies, you die. What's your name?"

"Mase," she said absently. "Listen, you can't get away with . . ." But even she could see that was an unproductive line of reasoning. She paused, and cleared her throat. "I can't stop him, now."

"I think you'll be surprised at what you can do with a laser at your back, Mase."

"You're bluffing. Colonials aren't allowed to carry lasers."

"Some of us manage. Like Garrett, over there. The one who's going to sign your death warrant if you don't stop him." I moved the weapon just a little. "I don't think a sample through this portion of your anatomy would prove fatal, if you'd like to experiment."

She drew in her breath. "No. I—I believe you."

Beside her, the florid insurance salesman had figured out that something was wrong. He was still working on what to do about it. Mase/McCormick cast a pitiable glance his way, but when he started to look over her shoulder at me, I said, "Eyes front, or she dies." He believed me. I returned my attention to Mase. "Stop Garrett."

"Honestly I don't think I can. He's, he's a little mad, I think, I don't know whether he'll respond . . ."

"I think you'd best try it." I started edging her and the florid gentleman both in Garrett's direction. They moved unwillingly, but they moved.

By now, the Special Service people had figured out that something was going on, and I expect their initial impulse was to kill a Colonial or two in the general area of the disturbance; Earthers are like that. The politician who had been speaking must have sensed trouble, too, because he faltered and looked around uncomfortably. I saw him only peripherally; my primary concern was the activity or lack thereof of one Garrett, Colonial, with delusions of competence and a laser to make them come true. If Mase didn't say something pretty damn quick, it would be too late.

The Special Service didn't bother me; having

determined that I must be the problem and that they couldn't kill me without endangering an Earther named Mase, they chose instead to float protectively toward the President, which was exactly what I'd hoped they would do. Maybe by accident one of them would get between her and Garrett.

Mase still didn't say anything. I guess I shouldn't have figured her for a totally gutless wonder; you don't get to be a high muckymuck in any government organization without showing some evidence of courage, I suppose, or at least competence. But there was still a chance I could stop Garrett, and at least Mase made a passable barrier between me and the Special Service.

"Garrett," I said. I couldn't wait any longer; aware that something was going on, but uncertain whether it concerned him, he was reaching for his weapon. "Don't touch it; the Special Service will kill you before you can fire. Mase or McCormick or whatever she called herself when she hired you was lying. Do you understand? She lied to you. You were never meant to kill the President." He looked startled, and glanced uncertainly around the chamber, which was suddenly very quiet. "In fact," I said, "you probably can't kill the President. You've been set up. Oh, I don't say Mase wouldn't have been glad to see you succeed, because I think she would have been; but you'll serve her purpose every bit as well if you die in the attempt. You were meant to die, of course." At least he was listening, and he wasn't reaching for the weapon anymore. "It's another gambit like the so-called terrorists, Garrett. Those were Mase/McCormick's idea, too. She wants war, and she wants it to look like we started it. But that isn't what she told you, is it?"

He looked at her mournfully. "But." His voice almost broke on the single syllable. "But you're a C.I.D. officer. I took it for granted that your word was good. You said the President was behind all that. You said if I killed her . . . You said I should kill her. You said." He sounded like a small child cheated of his rightful due.

The chamber got even quieter, after that. But not for long.

CHAPTER TWENTY-FIVE

When the florid gentleman finally figured out what to do, he did it well. It wasn't the best location in the world to hold a battle, with all those noncombatants in the way, fully half of them armed, and none of them agreed on a course of action. Fortunately, the armed contingent, with the exception of the Special Service people, were all Colonials, and Colonials don't fire at random into crowds. A lot of weapons were drawn, but none got used except mine.

It was all pretty spectacular, nonetheless. The florid gentleman took action with some skill and enthusiasm, doing what Mase/McCormick should have done in the first place: trying to disarm me. I stunned Mase, and gave the gentleman a considerable struggle till we reached Garrett's side and I could relinquish my stun gun in favor of his laser.

Garrett just floated, bewildered, out of the way. The Special Service people had their weapons drawn and aimed, but they still hadn't a clear shot at me, and maybe by now they were less certain whether I was the proper target. Anyway, I hoped they were.

The florid man and I might have been alone in the chamber, for all the attention either of us paid anyone else. I kept him between me and the Special Service people, but aside from that I ignored them. He went to Mase, to be sure she wasn't dead. Then he looked from me to her and back again in a helpless, puzzled way that I found startling after his competence in struggling with me. "You didn't have to stun her," he said.

"She'll get over it," I said. "She'll live long enough to stand trial for treason."

"Treason!" He sounded genuinely startled; clearly the word had never occurred to him in connection with what he and Mase were doing. "But . . . I mean . . . We weren't . . ."

"What's your name?" I asked gently.

"Lander," he said absently. Catch them by surprise and they seem to hand out their true names quite willingly. I never did find out why Mase had given us a false name when we first met her.

"Well, Lander, if what you were planning wasn't treason, what was it, exactly?" I tried to keep my tone gentle, even asking that. Now that Mase had been put out of action, Lander was reacting very like a child caught misbehaving with the big boys. Half frightened, half defiant, mostly just puzzled and hurt.

"Well, we, I mean," he said, and looked helplessly around the chamber. We were getting even more concentrated attention from the muckymucks than the verbose politician had got. "She said, I, I, we thought." He took a deep breath and turned suddenly away from me, his weapon forgotten in his hand, to face the President.

The Special Service guys hadn't forgotten his weapon, and they tried to interpose their bodies between Lander and the President, but she gestured them aside, watching him with interest and genuine concern. She was quite a lady.

"Everybody knows there's going to be another war; sir," Lander told her. "Mase . . . Well. We've got to, that is . . . I know it sounds a little crazy, sir, maybe it is a little crazy, Mase has been . . . but that's not important. She believes, she honestly believes that we can't wait, sir. That if we don't, well, *start* the war, you know, sir, that . . . that we have to start the war, of course making it look like Colonials did it, because if we wait, they'll take us by surprise, sir, we'll lose. I'm sorry, sir. I didn't really think she'd let him kill you. I thought . . . I thought there must be . . ." He paused, and sighed, and remembered the weapon in his hand. "Oh, sorry, sir." He let it go, perhaps expecting it to fall to the floor. Earthers *will* try to put things "down" in freefall.

I caught the weapon and holstered it. The Special Service people took Lander, Mase, and Garrett into custody. The rest of the muckymucks started to make some kind of fuss over what had happened: I fled the chamber before they could involve me.

Collis jiggled his cereal container without much interest. The President, who had invited us to breakfast, showed as little interest in her food as Collis did in his. "I'm so glad to meet you at last," she told me. "I've heard so many stories, and I have to admit, you've become something of a hero to me."

I think I blushed. I know my response was incoherent.

"Skyrider doesn't like for people to say stuff like that," said Collis. "She's just like my dad: they do all these exciting things and then they don't want anybody to talk about them, but I always want to, because it's exciting, don't you think, sir?''

The President smiled at him. "I certainly do." She looked at his cereal. "You know, you don't have to eat that if you don't want to."

He looked relieved. "I wasn't sure. I mean, 'cause you're the President and everything, sir."

"I distinctly remember telling you, the first time we played Planets together, that you're never to treat me like the President except in public," she said with mock sternness.

"Are you going to give her a reward for saving your life?"

"Collis!"

"It's all right, my dear," said the President. She winked at Collis. "Of course I am. That's why she did it, don't you know? Because she knew she could expect adequate recompense. The Skyrider doesn't do that sort of thing for the fun of it." She looked at me. There was a distinct twinkle of laughter in her eyes. "What would you like? Credits? Another shuttle? A rock of your own? Tell me. If I have it, it's yours."

"Just like that?" I asked, startled.

"Just like that." She smiled again. "I wouldn't ever want you to hesitate to save my life, should the need arise again, because you thought the pay had not been adequate the last time.

I hadn't really thought about it. I hadn't expected to be asked; and there wasn't really anything I needed.

She must have sensed my confusion. "Don't worry about it, my dear," she said. "Credits will be deposited to your account. And if you ever need anything more—anything at all—don't hesitate to come to me." She unfastened herself abruptly from her chair and floated out of it. "And now, I'm sorry, but I'm afraid duty calls. I'm supposed to be at the summit meeting, you know. They're discussing the hostage reports, and the tapes Jamin brought back. That agency will be disbanded, of course, but you know how politicians are. They can't ever just *do* something. First they have to talk it to death." She hesitated, looking at us very seriously. "Credits don't mean much, I know. I hope you realize how very grateful I am to you all. I don't suppose we can avert this war forever, but . . ." She smiled suddenly, shrugged, thanked us again, and left the chamber.

"I don't feel good," said Collis.

The number of credits deposited to my account was startling. But she was right: credits didn't mean much. They couldn't buy Collis permanent health in freefall, nor Jamin health in gravity, and they couldn't help avert the war or buy happiness or provide immortality or rid the world of rockdust or overcome inertia.

They could, however, provide a few creature comforts and a lot of fun for a battered old mercenary who liked a good old-fashioned game of Planets with the standard board and malite chips for markers.

We had moved Collis and both shuttles to a gravity station when we realized what was wrong with the boy: the medication that was supposed to keep him healthy in freefall wasn't working anymore. He'd seen it coming, of course; that was why it bothered him when I mentioned that being able to share an environment with his father would ease our minds should the war finally come.

While Jamin couldn't survive gravity forever, at

least he could endure it in moderation, so a gravity station was the logical place to stay while we waited for the med-techs to admit that Collis could never survive freefall after all. I even found a mutant med-tech who rebuilt my hand without discussing all the gory details. And I ordered a little work done on Jamin's shuttle.

When Collis was released from Sick Bay for the trip home to the Belt, he was planning to ride in the *Defiance* with me. Jamin's shuttle, newly painted and registered in his name, hadn't separate gravity quarters when we got her, and Collis had seen before what it did to his father to spend too much time in gravity. He didn't want to be responsible for that again.

"Will you mind making the trip in gravity, and having Collis along?" asked Jamin.

"I won't have him," I said.

He stared at me. We were on our way to the flight deck, and he tripped over a loose cable in the corridor, he was so busy staring at me. After just a short time in gravity he had already taken on again that cold look of aloof detachment that had made me think, when I first met him, that he was an arrogant ex-military jock with no redeeming qualities. I had been wrong.

"Watch where you're walking," I said. "Why should I? Have him with me, I mean. You're perfectly capable of taking him in your shuttle—what are you going to name her, by the way?—that is what we got her for after all. So the *Defiance* wouldn't be so crowded."

"Skyrider, he can't go all that way in gravity again," said Collis, oblivious to his father's efforts to shush him.

"I'll be fine," Jamin said stiffly.

"Well, if you're not," I said, "you can send Collis to his quarters and turn off the gravity."

"You know perfectly well," said Jamin.

"Why?" asked Collis, more to the point.

"Because your quarters have separate gravity controls."

"They didn't have, before, did they, Papa?"

"They have now," I said.

"But," said Jamin.

"It's entirely a matter of self-preservation," I said. "You needn't think I did it for your sakes. I want peace and quiet on the *Defiance*, and I'm not a damn babysitter."

"But it must have cost," began Jamin.

"Of course it cost," I said impatiently. "That's what credits are for. Besides, I still have enough left to stake me to a lifetime game of Planets, if I want. I'm rich."

"Sometimes gamblers lose," Collis said thoughtfully.

"Sure, sometimes they lose," I said. "And sometimes they win. That's why it's called gambling."

"And people like her think they'll always win," said Jamin. There was an odd note in his voice I didn't quite understand.

"Nobody can always win," said Collis.

"I don't know." Jamin grinned at him. "Maybe the Skyrider can."

"You damn betcha," I said.

GORDON R. DICKSON

HARRY HARRISON